Story by
NISIOISIN

JUNI TAISEN: ZODIAC WAR

Art by
HIKARU
NAKAMURA

Story by
NISIOISIN

JUNI TAISEN:
ZODIAC WAR

Art by
**HIKARU
NAKAMURA**

Translated by **NATHAN A. COLLINS**

viz media
SAN FRANCISCO

CONTENTS

THE FIRST BATTLE

*"Even a wild boar will become a
pig after seven generations."*

**INŌNOSHISHI,
THE FIGHTER
OF THE BOAR**

"I wish for love."

REAL NAME: **Toshiko INŌ**
BORN: **April 4**
HEIGHT: **176 cm**
WEIGHT: **60 kg**

Toshiko is the heiress of a distinguished family with a history that goes back over three centuries. She grew up caught between her father, whose parenting style was so severe some would call it abusive, and her mother, who took doting to new extremes. In time Toshiko learned how to appease them both in equal measure. As a child, all her focus went toward ascertaining what adults wanted of her, and once she attained adulthood herself, she became a free spirit—especially when it came to the one matter both her parents had rigidly denied her: romance.

Originally, her sister, five years her elder, had earned the right to participate in the Twelfth Zodiac War, but in the culmination of a twelve-year plot, Toshiko killed her sister and claimed the invitation for herself.

Her weapons of choice are two machine guns—one for each hand—named *Aishū* and *Inochigoi*. She is well versed in heavy weaponry, and nothing is too heavy for her to handle, but those two in particular she wields as if they are extensions of her own body.

She is currently in relationships with twelve different men but is still looking to take on more.

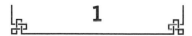

1

Inōnoshishi, the Fighter of the Boar, entered the abandoned high-rise near the center of the ghost town and thought, *My, for a derelict, this place is pristine.* It was unusual, yes, but not unexpected. Until a very short time ago, the building hadn't been abandoned, and the city hadn't been a ghost town. For the mere purpose of holding the Twelfth Zodiac War, and for no other reason, the battle organizers had wiped out an entire city. Boar thought, somewhat ruefully, *Not even my esteemed family wields the power to easily eliminate an entire metropolitan region of five hundred thousand in a single night.*

Such were Boar's thoughts as she strode through the building with grace—always with grace, and with elegance. The time written on the invitation had long since passed, but that was no reason for her to hurry. Rather, she held a deep conviction that the duty of the high class was to make others wait for them. *Besides,* she thought, *isn't it tradition for the Boar to appear last? The previous Boar's victory makes me in essence the defending champion, and I mustn't behave in an unbecoming manner.*

She tightened her fingers around the grips of the machine guns she held in either hand. She was determined and ready to kill. Boar had been taught to leave her hands free and ready to move in case of any contingency, but she adapted that lesson in her own way. If she was to be prepared for any contingency, wasn't it better to have a gun in each hand?

She wasn't now carrying these two massive machine guns only for this occasion. Aishū and Inochigoi—Lost Love and No Mercy—were always with her. She had even been granted legal dispensation to carry them at all times. Should anyone report her to the police, that person would be arrested, not her. Such was her stature as heiress to the great Inō family.

Not that any of the warriors gathering here today will be so easily intimidated, she thought. *Or will they?*

In essence, Boar was on the inside exactly who she appeared to be—haughty and domineering, generally unpleasant and ill-natured. But she wasn't a fool, nor was she reckless. She wasn't about to shut herself into the confined space of an elevator for an entire half-minute or longer. She took the stairs instead, and as she ascended the 150 flights, she never stopped refining her battle plans. That she needed to win was a given; what mattered was achieving that victory with elegance. A victory won through sweat was the same as losing. Her thoughts were solely occupied with how to kill her eleven formidable adversaries with the utmost refinement, in accordance with her venerable lineage.

The top floor opened onto a large space seemingly designed to offer a view of the nightscape far below. Entering this indoor observation deck, Boar announced, "Good evening, everyone. I trust your wait has been pleasant. I am Boar."

The view might have been something a few days ago, but the ghost town distant beneath them now offered only total darkness. While Boar certainly knew how to appreciate looking down from on high, the shadowy void wasn't even worth sparing a single glance. Besides, of far more pressing importance was sizing up the eleven fighters—already present—

with whom she was about to engage in mortal combat. None rose to meet her, and no response met her greeting. Rather, the fighters had dispersed throughout the room to keep themselves as far apart from one another as possible. A table located in the center of the space offered an extravagant buffet, as if this were some fancy dinner party, but no one was eating, and no one was conversing. The atmosphere was so potently oppressive that an average person might buckle under the pressure of just being there. But to Boar, the sensation was a thing to be savored, and she lightly licked her lips as if to taste it.

More familiar faces here than I expected, she thought. As she examined her adversaries, her expression remained blank, save for the faint smirk she maintained in duty to her status. *Ox… and Sheep. Chicken, and Dog. Ah, and this one—I've never seen her in person before, but she must be Tiger. And there's Monkey. Well, I suppose that unpleasant woman was bound to be here. Now, that kid sleeping against the wall…him, I don't know.*

Then she noticed the severed head, the stump of the neck dark red; it must have been cut free with a very sharp blade. Not letting the surprise reach her expression, she moved only her eyes and searched for the matching body and immediately found it, as it too had been casually discarded on the floor. There was no art to be found in the sight, just a severed head and a toppled corpse. Boar had thought the room's mood seemed heavy, even considering the killings that would soon commence, and this, it appeared, was the cause.

Looks like one fighter was so careless, he got himself killed before we even started. Apparently, something had gone down before she arrived. She glanced at the decidedly odd-looking man standing closest to the corpse.

"Hmm?" the man said, tilting his head as if Boar's arrival had only now reached his attention. "I didn't do it. It wasn't me. Don't go accusing anyone when you don't have any proof."

He pointed at her with a large, blood-soaked blade, the gesture too casual to be intended as a threat. It was as if he meant to point a finger at her, and his hand just happened to be holding a sword. To this man, pointing a finger and pointing a sword were the same thing. Since Boar considered her machine guns to be just another part of her body, the two warriors shared this common understanding, if little else. Another unsettling convergence came from the second sword he held in his other hand. Something akin to two long-bladed hatchets, the twin weapons possessed a matching size, design, and menace. *Two swords, meet two machine guns.*

Not that this should suggest the two fighters shared any affinity. His second sword was still pristine, but she sensed that if he got any closer to her, he wouldn't hesitate to paint that shiny metal red to match.

Proof? Boar thought. *I'm pretty sure that blood-drenched blade is proof enough.* Before she could decide if the man was attempting to provoke her or if he was just plain crazy, a voice spoke.

"Welcome, fighters."

A silk-hatted old man was standing at a window with the blotted-out skyline at his back. No sound had betrayed his arrival. No opening door, no footstep—it was as if he had been there the entire time. All eyes turned to him, save for those of the sleeping youth, who showed no sign of awakening.

"Now that everyone has arrived," the old man continued, "we shall commence the Twelfth Zodiac War. Everybody, clap your hands!"

He applauded vigorously. To what was surely no one's surprise, none of the combatants joined in.

Unperturbed by the chilly reception, the man went on. "I am Duodecuple, and I've been given the honor of being your referee for this great battle. Pleased to make your acquaintances."

The picture of humility and respect, Duodecuple offered a deep bow.

Well, I don't see myself ever pronouncing that name right, Boar thought, otherwise mostly uninterested in the man's arrival. He had interrupted—and spoiled—the tense moment between her and the sword-wielding man, who now seemed to have forgotten about her and was instead staring at Duodecuple with a strange gleam in his eyes. Some others might have taken the swordsman's demeanor as that of rapt attention, but Boar knew better—he was trying to decide whether or not he could kill the old man on the spot.

So, Boar thought, *he determines friend and foe according to whom he can and cannot kill. Surprise, surprise. I thought I'd be the only one here who worked that way.*

She wondered if the old man detected the menace hidden in the swordsman's stare.

Duodecuple said, "Without any further ado, let's go over the rules, shall we? If you please, direct your attention to the central table."

Somehow, the table had been cleared and the food replaced with twelve murky-black, jewel-like orbs. *Murky, but beautiful.* Each jewel was identical in size, color, and otherwise, but the significance of their number—twelve—was not lost on Boar.

"Everyone," the judge said, "please take one apiece."

Keeping their eyes on each other, the twelve fighters approached the table to collect their orbs.

Although, not all twelve—remaining motionless were the dead one, obviously, and the sleeping one too.

If that kid doesn't wake up, Boar thought, *he'll just lose via forfeit.*

But to her surprise, one combatant shook him awake on the way back from claiming an orb.

I see you're still refusing to mind your own business, Monkey.

Monkey and Boar hadn't shared the same battlefield in quite some time, but apparently the woman's meddlesome streak hadn't changed. After their last encounter, Boar figured that the next time the two met, one of them would die, and present circumstances called for no revision to that sentiment.

The jewel's murky black appeared darker up close. Rolling her jewel in her fingers, Boar thought, *What surprises me is that, with all these fighters and all their apparent peculiarities, especially this dangerous one*—she glanced at the sword-wielding man—*they're each following to the letter the instructions of this so-called judge, a man we've never seen or heard before. I guess that just goes to show how major an event this Zodiac War is. I mean, I knew that going in, but one can't really comprehend it until one's here.*

Without a token word of thanks to Monkey, the awakened boy sleepily claimed his orb. Now only one remained unclaimed.

"Hey, Mr. Judge guy," one fighter said, raising his hand. "Since my brother's orb is left over, I don't see there's any problem in my taking it, is there?"

When Boar turned her attention to the face of the man who was so brazenly attempting to gain a leg-up on his competition, what she saw startled her. His face was a nearly identical match to the one on the severed head, which by now was drawing no particular notice. There were differences in expression, of course—one was animated and the other frozen in an anguished death grimace—but once seen, the similarities were unmistakable.

Were they twins? Boar wondered. Both had similar-looking tanks strapped onto their backs—perhaps some kind of weapon. *Twin fighters... Could they be those criminals, the Tatsumi Brothers?*

Though some might have been offended by the man caring more about the worth of the jewels than the death of his twin brother, Duodecuple's response was placid. "Please, go ahead. I don't mind. Take it."

The twin scooped up the orb intended for his brother with a victorious laugh. "How about that? Score!"

"However," Duodecuple continued. "I'm going to have to ask you to swallow only one."

"Wait, what? Swallow? This thing?"

"Yes. And that goes for all of you. Please swallow your jewels—without biting them, mind you. Water has been provided should you need it."

Boar hesitated, not because she desired her jewel for its value—she had never wanted for money—but the size of the thing held her back for a moment. But when the swordsman swallowed his, followed by the sleeping youth, and then Monkey, Boar sensed this was no time for indecision. This battle might have just been starting, but it *had* started. Any open sign of fear would designate her the first target. Besides, her pride wouldn't allow such a public display of cowardice.

"Has everyone swallowed their jewels?" Duodecuple asked, surveying the room. "All right, allow me to explain what they are. Those little orbs are a kind of crystallized poison. We call them beast gems. When ingested by a human, they undergo a unique chemical reaction with gastric acid and become fatal in roughly twelve hours."

This might have been a shocking announcement, but of the eleven combatants, none reacted with surprise. As soon as they had been told to swallow the jewels—if not sooner—they all recognized the gems weren't there to improve their health. Boar hadn't figured out the tasteless crystal was poison, but when the reveal came, her thoughts were along the lines of, *Yeah, that makes sense.* If anything, it was anticlimactic.

The twin who had claimed his brother's spare orb said, "Damn, I'm not going to get any money for poison," but he still pocketed it in a shrewd move that belied his superficial front.

Duodecuple continued, "The jewels have been shaped in such a way that regurgitation is impossible. My deepest apologies for the inconvenience. Now that that's out of the way, let's go over the basic rules. I won't repeat them, so please listen attentively. That said, the rules have been simplified this time around, and there should be no room for confusion. The Eleventh Zodiac War got a little overly complicated, and we're not above recognizing when we've made a mistake."

"The fighter who collects all twelve orbs will be the victor and will be granted a single wish—any wish at all."

Simple indeed. But it did leave some room for questions. Whether or not Boar wanted to do the asking herself, she wasn't sure. If possible, she would have liked to observe the other combatants asking—depending on who asked and the questions they raised, she might be able to glean crucial information about her adversaries for the coming death match. Now was an opportunity to find out something about the natures of the fighters she hadn't yet met.

Unfortunately, the first inquiry came from a fighter she already knew well—Ox.

Well, what fighter wouldn't know "the Natural"?

"Mr. Duodecuple, sir," Ox said, correctly pronouncing the judge's name, "if we've all taken poison, doesn't that mean that win or lose, we're all going to die?"

Ox was a distinctly morose man with black hair almost as long as he was tall—and he was undoubtedly a favorite to win. Boar thought him foolish for asking the question as soon as it came to him, without regard for strategy. On the other hand, he'd never needed to resort to trickery to win a battle.

"An obvious question," Duodecuple replied. "I hope the obvious answer will suffice. You need not be concerned. The victor will be provided the antidote. Consider it a bonus prize."

In other words, it was win or die. And not only that, but becoming the sole survivor wasn't good enough on its own—complete victory had to come within twelve hours, or the antidote might come too late. If anyone was going to survive this battle, he or she needed to secure the win within the allotted time. Considering the caliber of the chosen fighters, this was not going to be a simple task.

But that's not the real issue...

As if finishing Boar's thought, Ox asked, "You said that the orbs react to stomach acid, right? That means that they'll dissolve in our stomachs?"

"That is correct," the judge responded, "and astute as well. The exact rate of absorption will vary slightly from person to person, but the process is one-way and absolute. As the time limit approaches, the jewels will begin to shrink and eventually disappear."

If the poison should completely dissolve in the stomach of just one fighter, no one could win. No matter how you counted it, eleven capsules weren't going to be enough.

"Might I add another question?"

It was Sheep who'd spoken up now. He was a small old man, and unfortunately for Boar, another fighter already known to her—although she had understood him to be retired.

He might be older than even Duode...whoever, Boar thought, her internal monologue stumbling over the judge's name. *Sheep is practically a legend. Not only did I assume he had retired, I half expected him to be dead by now. I hate to complain, but his being here is going to be a problem.*

Sheep continued, "My combat style is...how could I put it? A bit fierce, I'd say. This isn't the time or place to show my hand, of course, but you see, I've come prepared to utilize some high explosives, should the need arise. Of course, I'll try to avoid such occasions, but what happens if, contrary to my intentions, I happen to destroy an orb in the process of obtaining it?"

For supposedly not showing his hand, the old man had gone out of his way to make it clear he had explosives. Hiding the attempt at intimidating the other fighters behind a question was a crafty ploy from a veteran conniver.

That's just what I despise about him. But I could ask the question about my machine guns too. The ammo could easily shatter such jewels.

"Have no fear," the judge said. "The poison gems will only react with fresh human stomach acid. Nothing else can harm them—no matter how destructive the physical force may be. If you would like, you may test it for yourself."

"No, no," Sheep said. "There's no need for that. Your word is good enough for me." No need to press the issue—his question had achieved its intended purpose. Besides, this was the Zodiac War, and its combatants would be bringing a grand assortment of destructive forces beyond explosives and bullets. The organizers wouldn't have prepared gems so easily broken.

"I have one last question," Ox said, reclaiming control of the discussion. "We've all put these durable little gems into our bodies. How are we supposed to collect them now?"

Duodecuple replied, "I'll leave the method up to your own abilities and judgments, but if I might offer a suggestion, I would think slitting open the stomach to be the simplest solution."

2

With a bow simultaneously fawning and snobbish, the judge of the Zodiac War said, "You are all world-class fighters, tenacious and resilient. May you find the victory you seek." And then he was gone—as if he had never been there at all.

Then, just as Boar began considering how she could best seize the upper hand, another fighter spoke up, interrupting her thoughts.

"Everyone, may I have your attention?"

It was Monkey.

She had clearly caught the other fighters off guard and easily claimed the first move. She spoke with a congenial smile vastly out of place amid the tense atmosphere that only thickened after Duodecuple's speech.

"I have a proposal," she said. "Under the rules of this Zodiac War, none of us need to die—as long as we all cooperate."

Such a ridiculous suggestion hardly came as a surprise from Monkey. Boar could all too easily see what the woman was thinking.

How magnanimous, as always. She's surely scheming up some kind of collusion, like deciding on a winner who will then use their one and only wish to bring everyone else back to life. Just like her to sell an obvious idea as if it were something brilliant. As if anyone would waste a precious wish on something so frivolous as reviving the others.

"Can I count on anyone to cooperate?"

What is this, a charity drive? Boar felt herself getting angry at Monkey's tone, but then let it go. Whether or not Monkey was being genuine, the woman was making herself stand out. She had placed herself squarely in the middle of the other fighters' crosshairs. While the other fighters focused on taking Monkey out, Boar could take her sweet time perfecting her plan of action.

Then one hand slowly made its way upward. Someone was actually offering to join her.

It was the sleepy youth.

Come on, kid, can't you see the opening she's handing to you? What kind of warrior are you?

Even now the boy's head sagged and jolted back up, as if he might fall back asleep at any moment. "I'd like nothing better," he said, his speech torpid and halting—more like talking in his sleep than anything else, "than to get through this... without anyone dying."

Boar started to get the feeling she'd heard his voice somewhere, but no actual memories stirred, even when he continued. "But let me guess your plan...You want us to make you the winner...then you'll bring us all back to life?"

It was a plan easier said than done. As for the familiarity of his voice, Boar chalked it up to just her imagination.

"That's not quite what my plan is," Monkey replied, her cheerful voice buoyed by the show of support. "If we do it that way, some of you might harbor doubts that I will hold up my end. My method comes with better assurances."

Hmph. All right, maybe she used that monkey brain to actually think about this.

As much as she derided the woman in her thoughts, Boar hadn't a clue as to Monkey's plan. Despite holding an unquenchable hatred toward the serial meddler, Boar certainly didn't discount her as a threat, and she knew she had to do more than just stand by and watch this development.

But while Boar was contemplating the situation, two more raised their hands, one after the other, to join the sleepy youth.

This is bad. Now Ox and Chicken are joining in.

Then another slowly lifted his hand—a massive man unknown to Boar. With the boy and Monkey, that made five. Nearly half the assembled forces. The youth had probably joined in out of gratitude toward Monkey for waking him up, or some other equally childish reason, but his actions had prodded the fighters from merely scoping each other out into suddenly taking action. Simply watching and letting this happen was a failure Boar could never undo. Whether or not Monkey's scheme could succeed, this battle royale was about to start with nearly half the players forming an alliance. Any way Boar looked at it, this was not good news to her. Worse yet was Ox's presence in their number—even alone, he posed a major threat.

I have to do something to stop this right now. One more hand, and their alliance will number six out of eleven.

But to unleash two machine guns with reckless abandon and plunge the room into chaos would not be principled. To remain true to herself required fighting with elegance and style.

Fortunately, Boar didn't have to do anything. A sixth fighter raised his hand. Rather, he raised a blood-stained sword. It was the sword-wielding man with the menacing stare. In quick response, Ox, Chicken, and the giant quietly lowered their hands. The sword-wielder's participation had driven three from the armistice plan. Boar wasn't surprised. Even if that man's sword had been clean of blood, he gave off such an unmistakable aura of danger that anyone who failed to notice it could hardly be considered a fighter.

"All right," Monkey said. "Thank you. I'm just happy that two other peace-seekers are here. Everyone else—if you ever change your mind, you're always welcome to seek me."

In no conceivable scenario was that bladed man raising his arm with any form of sincerity, and here she was welcoming him. Was she so lacking a fighter's instincts? And that tired boy—did he keep his hand up because he felt it was too late to withdraw?

Monkey continued, "Now, why don't you two come over here, and we can—"

Movement. Someone other than Boar must have decided this had gone on long enough. Perhaps that person considered a team of three to be still a team that needed to be broken up before it could form.

It happened so suddenly Boar couldn't tell who had done it, or how, but the next instant the floor split apart.

To the surprise of everyone but the mystery instigator, the fighters found the ground separate from their feet. As each recovered from their shock, they responded to the sudden forced descent in their own ways.

The Twelfth Zodiac War was on.

3

When Boar landed on the floor below amid the cascade of debris, the other fighters had already scattered. Only she had chosen to land with as much poise as possible; the others seemed to have prioritized using the chaos to leave the scene undetected.

How so very smart of them, Boar thought.

As long as there was a time limit, the fighters couldn't stay concealed forever, but neither would anyone who qualified for this prestigious battle be pressured into acting rashly.

I don't know who broke apart the floor, but whoever it is, I'd better be on my guard. Either they have some superhuman power, or they arrived early to set a trap.

Whatever the case, collapsing the floor was a big move that stopped Team Monkey before it could form. That a team held an advantage was an obvious truth—it was a simple numbers game—but to someone like Boar the concept of pacifism was so alien that even the idea of such a team was repellent. And if that sword-wielding man, clearly no pacifist himself, joined forces with Monkey and the drowsy boy, who knew what they would do?

Boar sensed that her first priority should be to kill Monkey before the alliance could reassemble and put into motion some plot. When she imagined what it would feel like to finally rid herself of that woman, Boar felt as if a load had lifted from her shoulders—and when she pictured herself tearing open Monkey's stomach, she even felt a carnal thrill.

But these thoughts were interrupted by the sense of another presence—not that sensing it was any great feat. The presence emanated such strong waves of pure evil that the nearby rubble and debris would probably roll right off the building in an attempt to escape, had they the ability to do so.

Boar turned to find the sword-wielding man standing there. He hadn't been there before—whether he had been under the rubble or if he had left and come back, she didn't know.

"I could have started with anyone, you know," the man said theatrically. "Wouldn't matter to me. But you falsely accused me, you see. So I figured I ought to settle this grudge. Going into a battle with a clouded head is no way to win, don't you think? The mental game is as important as anything, yeah? And you—you're a bad person, leveling accusations when you don't have no proof. Where's your humanity?"

Boar was speechless. Judging by his incoherent rambling, Boar doubted any hope remained for his mental game. But she didn't doubt his sincerity—it really could have been anyone he chose. The man came for her not out of any strategy, but because she had happened to leave an impression on him.

By informing her decision to arrive last, Boar's pursuit of gentility had made her his first target. Perhaps it would have been better for Boar had Team Monkey gotten off the ground, as this man would surely have turned his blades on Monkey instead. That was how flighty his targeting was.

I so wish it didn't have to be this way. To think I have to fight in Monkey's place. Even worse, it's almost like I'm protecting her.

As one part of Boar's mind thought along those lines, the rest turned an analytical eye to her opponent and sized him up. He was hardly the type of man she enjoyed observing in detail, but she wasn't about to go blindly into a fight just because her foe creeped her out.

Hmm…He's so peculiar, it's hard to get a good read on him, but I can tell he can fight. "Aura" is perhaps a word I prefer to reserve for those of a higher class, but he carries an air about him. Of all the fighters, only Ox and myself would stand a chance against him.

Whether she stood a chance or not, she wished she didn't have to fight him. She had hoped to let her stronger adversaries battle it out among themselves. But she had never left much to hoping. Luxury was to be made, not asked for—such was her philosophy. This was the time to rise to action—to graceful action.

I truly wish I didn't have to fight you so soon, but now you've chosen your death.

"I am Inōnoshishi, the Fighter of the Boar. I kill in abundance."

"I am Usagi, the Fighter of the Rabbit. I kill with distinction."

So he knew enough manners to properly introduce himself.

Boar readied her two machine guns, Aishū and Inochigoi, to fill her enemy with holes. If she were to believe Duodecuple, no matter how many holes her bullets punched through him, the gem would remain unharmed and intact. She could take her time sifting through the blood and meat to find it.

The sword-wielding man—Rabbit, apparently—raised his giant weapons and rushed at her in a bounding charge, but any way you looked at it, her bullets would be faster. Though the woman greatly admired the determination behind his unflinching attack in the face of her twin barrels, a blind charge was perhaps the worst move anyone could make against her.

Just as her fingers squeezed the triggers, someone was grabbing her arms from behind, pinning them to her back. She managed to fire, but her machine guns had been thrown off target. Not one bullet even grazed Rabbit.

But his swords did not miss.

The two blades skewered her and went right on through to whoever had seized her from behind.

For a moment, she wondered if he had gone for her heart. But no, it was her esophagus. This hadn't been some blind attack, but rather a precise incision to remove her gem. He had claimed her life with a familiar and methodical ease, as if he were merely opening the perforated plastic wrap of a pack of pocket tissues.

And he even stabbed his ally too…

In that brief moment he had disappeared after the floor's collapse, Rabbit had formed an alliance and staged an attack on Boar. She never would have imagined him to be so persuasive or sociable to pull it off, but what other explanation could there be?

And who was it? Who was so sneaky and so underhanded as to get behind me without my noticing and pin my arms?

Using all of her remaining strength, she twisted her neck to look over her shoulder. What she saw shocked her even more than the blades that had penetrated her esophagus. But it wasn't the face of the figure that surprised her. It couldn't have, because there was no face. There was no head at all.

What had grabbed her was a headless corpse—a corpse that until moments earlier had been on the floor. Sure enough, it would have come down with the rest of the rubble.

"You—you," Boar said as blood flooded the edges of her eyes. She turned her head forward. No more time to choose the most elegant words. "You're a necromancer!"

"No, a necromanticist," Rabbit said, pulling his blades free of the woman and the corpse. "I can make friends with people I've killed."

No wonder she hadn't sensed the thing creeping up behind her. He was already dead.

"That's the Fighter of the Snake, by the way," Rabbit said, entirely amicable. "I'm sorry I lied about not killing him. It was just a precaution. You see, I thought you might be aware of my abilities. I didn't want you to think I'd brought him to my side."

He hadn't fooled her, of course. Not that she had any breath left to say so.

I can't believe this is my end.

The proud woman brought to total disgrace, Boar slumped lifelessly to the floor. The last words she heard, before that thing within that defined her as her drifted away, drove the fallen warrior not to shame but to despair.

"Please forgive me, all right? Because from now on, you'll be my friend too."

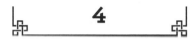

4

And with that, only moments after the start of the Zodiac War, the representative for the previous contest's winning sign met with defeat—and Rabbit's corpse alliance was born.

RABBIT VS. ~~BOAR~~
END OF THE 1ˢᵀ BATTLE

THE SECOND BATTLE

"Crow like a chicken, steal like a dog."

**DOKKU,
THE FIGHTER
OF THE DOG**

"I wish to win."

REAL NAME: **Michio TSUKUI**
BORN: **May 5**
HEIGHT: **177 cm**
WEIGHT: **52 kg**

Michio doesn't believe in fighting with weapons and instead prefers to bite his opponents. His vicious teeth, capable of pulverizing anything, have been called the "Mad Dog's Vise," which is greatly feared.

He works as a daycare teacher and, by all accounts, earns raves from parents and kids alike, but in secret, his real profession is finding children who possess certain gifts and delivering them to the organizations who want them. When, due to an oversight, he once let a little girl slip into the hands of a man who was nothing more than a pedophile, Michio risked his life to rescue her. He took her in as his adopted daughter and works hard both at daycare and on the battlefield to earn enough money to give her a proper upbringing.

In his personal time, he is an avid calligrapher. At first his works earned little regard, but through perseverance and practice, in time he acquired a bold, masterful brushwork that silenced all his detractors.

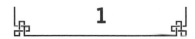

1

The Zodiac War was not confined to any specific area. The starting point had been located in a high-rise in the center of a city abandoned solely for this purpose, but once begun, the battle could go anywhere—even, for example, across borders. In fact, the previous Boar, who won the Zodiac War twelve years prior, deliberately brought the battle into a large, densely populated city and embroiled tremendous numbers of innocent bystanders in the fight.

Dokku, the Fighter of the Dog thought, *The way Boar created an advantage by using the mass confusion and riots as a shield—I could learn a thing or two from that. Not that I'll be able to use that same strategy this time. With this time limit, we're not going to be able to stray far from where we are. Even though we separated at the start, we all share the same interest in remaining in close enough proximity to stay in the fight.*

And so, rather than follow the example set by the previous winner, Dog chose the opposite approach. He decided to bide his time and hid in a secluded location where he could keep distance from the other fighters and remain safe from discovery. With his bared fangs, he made for a brutal, savage figure—and in truth, he had that side as well—but he was also shrewd and cool-headed.

When you think you know what to do, sometimes you need to do the opposite.

Because this Zodiac War had a considerable number of eager combatants, Dog thought it would be more prudent to let them slug it out among themselves and to only take action himself once their numbers were whittled down and less could be left to chance. While Dog possessed the strong pride of a warrior, and he believed he could best each and every one of the other fighters by his own strength, he resisted that temptation. He could keep his pride in check to find a more certain victory.

I shouldn't have to worry about Rabbit, judging by how he killed Snake before the battle had even begun. He's nothing more than a killer, and he doesn't have what it takes to survive a Zodiac War. That leaves Ox as the biggest problem...

Aside from Ox, the only fighter who concerned Dog was whoever had blown apart the floor. That trick caught all the other combatants off guard—Dog included. But who was it? Dog knew he shouldn't act until he learned the answer.

Well, I'll wait. That's my prerogative. Deep down, every dog wants to wait. And that's what I'll do, until we're down to three fighters at the most.

But this logic wasn't the only reason Dog was so ready to accept settling in and waiting out the Zodiac War. There was another, more dominant reason, relating to the rules of the game—specifically, the conditions for victory. Though the rules had been as much of a surprise to him as to anyone else, they served him better than he could have ever wished for.

The fighters had all ingested their jewels and now had to claim them from each other. Unless they got their own jewels out, the protective coating would dissolve and the poison would begin eating them from within. Duodecuple explained that the poison would kill them in twelve hours, but certainly they wouldn't all drop dead at the exact same moment. Not even the organizers of this grand event were capable of formulating a capsule with such time-bomb precision for each individual fighter. No, as time passed, the poison would work its way into every corner of their bodies. Dog suspected that after ten hours, the act of fighting would become difficult. Furthermore, the effectiveness of any poison differed from person to person. Some might even begin to show the effects even earlier—and it was that fear that would pressure the fighters into avoiding the cautious play that was typical of the early stages of Zodiac Wars past.

But Dog was different.

Because when Dog fought, his weapon of choice was poison.

He'd led the world to believe his signature style to be his powerful bite delivered by the so-called Mad Dog's Vise, when in reality his weapon of choice was the poison that coated his fangs. The secret wasn't so hard to hide when all who had encountered it did him the favor of dying.

His body could naturally produce a variety of toxins that, when introduced into his enemies, produced effects ranging from death to more death. The process did involve biting his victims, and by that measure, the public's image of him was not entirely baseless.

As an accomplished poisoner, Dog had immediately recognized the murky-black stone as a form of poison, and by the time he'd taken it into his mouth, his body was already at work producing the antidote. In other words, Dog was not currently poisoned. The jewel had been completely neutralized, and Dog was in full health. Forget twelve hours—Dog could remain here in wait for as long as his stamina allowed. The oppressive time limit would restrict the battle to the ghost city, but Dog alone was free from the rules of the game. Still, he knew he couldn't go too far if he wanted to strike at the right time.

This feels a little like cheating, but I'm not going to feel guilty over it. I'm going to use this advantage to the fullest.

At first, this position of privilege tempted him into thinking he might remain hidden until the very end, when any remaining fighters had been so ravaged by battle and poison they could hardly stand, and then he would arrive in peak fighting condition. But the situation he faced wasn't quite so ideal—if he waited until the very last moment, he would risk the poison jewels dissolving in his opponents' bodies entirely. Just as poisons affected different people in different ways, each person's stomach held differing levels of acidity. Once any jewel dissolved completely, reconstructing it would become an impossible feat, no matter how much of an expert with poison Dog was. He wasn't familiar with all his opponents, and there was no rule against a warrior having excess stomach acid.

And so, rather than wait for a certain amount of time to pass, Dog decided to stay in hiding until his opponents had been reduced in number. Until there were three fighters, or maybe fewer, he would stay here—here in this perfect hiding place, where no one would ever find him.

"I foooooound you," sang the voice.

2

Dog had chosen to hide in the underground parking lot of the same abandoned high-rise where the fighters had assembled, not because he thought it so close that no one would think to look there, but simply because it made for an ideal hiding spot due to the darkness and the great number of vehicles whose owners were no longer here—perhaps no longer anywhere. Rather, it *should* have made for an ideal hiding spot, but Dog had been found out before the first half hour had passed.

"I foooooound you," the voice had said in the sing-songy manner of a child playing hide-and-go-seek. But this was no child. This was a woman—a warrior. She was unknown to him, and she was hugging a trident-like weapon to her chest.

Shit! Dog thought, understandably panicked. The same qualities that made the underground garage an ideal hiding place also made it a disadvantageous arena. Between the darkness and restricted sightlines, Dog would have trouble putting his close-quarters biting style to good use. Even worse, it offered his foe free reign to wield her long, slender weapon.

And the battle is only just getting started, damn it. That slow-acting poison probably isn't having any effect on her at all.

Dog had hoped to face opponents who had been weakened from the toxic jewels, but now he was facing an enemy who was still at full strength.

He cast the doubts from his head and was beginning to rise to his feet when she said, her words tumbling out, "Ah! Oh, please don't misunderstand. I mean you no harm."

Here she was, standing before him, facing down at him, having him at a complete disadvantage, and she was stopping to explain herself.

"My-my name is Niwatori…of the Chicken, and I… I wanted to see if we could team up."

Team up? Dog reflexively furrowed his brows. *I guess she* did *respond to Monkey's offer.*

He recalled what had happened before the floor collapsed. Monkey was joined right away by that sleepy-looking boy… then Ox, then that giant man, and this woman. Dog's profession relied on reading people, and he turned his analytical eye on her. She seemed meek, yet her clothes were both gaudy and revealing. If anything, they felt like a costume she had been forced to wear. Was she not here because she wanted to be?

Dog asked, "You say you want to team up?"

"Y-yes," she answered. "Everything got left up in the air when we were scattered, but…" As she continued, her voice got quieter and quieter, as if she were losing the courage to speak. "But this is a battle royale, and I still think starting in teams is obviously the best idea. So, that's why…why I…"

Dog took this to mean that she hadn't been looking for him in particular. She'd only happened to find him first after the split, and she'd come with her guard down, hoping to form a team.

Didn't she stop to wonder why, if "starting in teams" was so "obvious," Monkey was the only one to initiate that move?

Chicken seemed to have not yet realized that a single winner meant that team play and betrayal came as two sides of the same coin. Maybe she had accepted Monkey's invitation not because she shared the same pacifist intentions, but rather out of a simplistic strategy born of short-term thinking.

"We can join forces," she explained, "until we're the last two left. Then we'll have a fair fight, one-on-one. It's as easy as that. So please, won't you join me?"

She seemed to earnestly believe it a mutually beneficial agreement to which refusal was inconceivable. But rather than accept right away, Dog thought it over.

He saw little benefit to be derived from teaming up with such a foolish girl—especially considering his unique advantage as a master of poison. On the other hand, responding to her offer with a flat refusal might turn this encounter into a fight he'd rather avoid. Though she might have been foolish and lacking in prudence, she was still an elite fighter chosen for the Zodiac War. Dog figured her prowess in battle must have been considerable to make up for her stupidity.

Even if Dog were to defeat her in combat, it wasn't guaranteed to be an easy fight. An injury in this early stage of the battle might upset his plans for the long game—and it was now, when his advantage was not yet actualized, that Dog was at the greatest risk of being eliminated.

He began forming a plan. *My best move might be to pretend to join her, then immediately steer us to a location where I can kill her before we happen upon any of the other fighters.*

It was a fiendish plan utterly lacking in humanity—in other words, a very human plan.

Then she added, "Please. We have to hurry. We're in danger. Terrible, terrible danger." Worry beset her face, leaving no trace of the warrior showing through. "The terrible, frightening man with the two long, giant hatchets, he—I can't even believe it—he's a necromanticist! He's killed Boar, and he already has a team of three!"

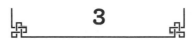

3

Niwatori, the Fighter of the Chicken, explained that she possessed a special power that had earned her a place among the twelve—or perhaps had been the reason she was forced into being there. She called the power her "Eye of the Cormorant." She could commune with all species of bird, and it was through that ability that she had found Dog in his underground hiding place.

Now that she mentioned it, Dog remembered seeing a pigeon perched on the ledge of a ceiling beam inside the car park. Wherever a bird could go, whether outside or indoors, was effectively within her field of view. Even if the organization behind the Zodiac Wars wielded enough power to clear an entire city of its residents, their reach didn't extend so far as to restrict any birds from flying in or out.

Just as Dog's powers over poison provided him a powerful advantage over the other fighters, so did Chicken's vision for her. Through her Eye of the Cormorant, she had witnessed the fight between Rabbit and Boar—and she had seen its end. With the help of Snake's corpse, Rabbit had killed Boar, then left with his two undead allies.

When Dog heard this, his first thought was, *She really is stupid.* No matter how badly Chicken felt compelled to tell someone about the spectacle she had witnessed, she should never have revealed the nature and extent of her special powers so openly to another fighter whom she'd only just met.

This was an incomprehensible lack of caution.

Her power was truly enviable and would have served as a tremendous boon to any fighter. If it were up for sale, he'd have been the first in line. But it would give her no advantage in close-quarters hand-to-hand combat. As long as he remained near her side, he could fight and win against her at any moment. He could kill her anytime he wanted to, and she posed no threat to him whatsoever. He could use her for all she was worth, and once he'd wrung every bit of advantage from her special abilities, he could kill her at his discretion. As long as he didn't wait too long, she'd be gone before she could ever stand in his way.

No, the problem now was Rabbit. What had Chicken called him—a necromanticist? To think that such a person existed. The more he killed, the more fighters he would have under his command. He was a killer and a creator. A creator and a horror. Such a power was superior to Chicken's, of course, but possibly even Dog's as well.

By turning his defeated opponents into his minions, this creator of the undead could construct an alliance that would never betray him. The obstacles other fighters faced in forming alliances—and the drawbacks in doing so—were practically nonexistent to him. He would never have to keep an eye over his shoulder for the moment his allies would turn on him, and the more he killed as the Zodiac War progressed, the larger his alliance would become. Theoretically, as a worst-case scenario, the fight might end up as eleven versus one. Even worse, Dog's talents as a master of poison would mean nothing against Rabbit's minions. No poison existed that could kill someone who was already dead. Although he didn't know it for sure, and wouldn't unless he tried, Dog suspected that biting those corpses and injecting his venom would have no effect at all. He would be forced to fight the former warriors in straight-up hand-to-hand combat.

If it comes to that, I'm already sunk, but just to make things worse, the poison jewels won't likely be having any effect on them either. Corpses don't produce stomach acid.

Rabbit's "allies" were free of the limits imposed by the deadline. Were they the only ones?

Chicken's Eye of the Cormorant, my ability to manipulate poison, and now Rabbit the necromanticist—this isn't happening by mere coincidence.

Dog was finding it more and more likely that the organizers of this Zodiac War had devised the rules and the setting to match the combatants' special powers. Each fighter held some advantage over one or another of the constraints of the battle. Victory would rely upon how they used their advantages.

Okay, so the rules aren't so simple as Duodecuple made them out to be. Now, what do I do about it?

Whatever Dog did, it would have to differ from what he had been doing. Putting aside the issue of how to deal with Chicken, he could no longer afford to hide until the Zodiac War's final stages. If Dog were to remain inactive, Rabbit would put his advantage in numbers to work as he and his minions coldly and systematically eliminated the other fighters. Worse, anyone they killed would join their ranks.

Everyone he defeats joins his side. What is this, a boys' manga?

It took no great leaps of imagination for Dog to picture what would happen when he finally emerged from hiding only to find Rabbit and his minions—if not eleven strong, then at least seven or eight.

All those fighters, with all their distinctive traits, under his
absolute command... Just because it's easy to imagine, it's not any
less chilling to think about.

No, if Dog was to act, he needed to do it soon. Now, even.
He needed to put a stop to Rabbit while the killer still had
only two corpses at his beck and call. Dog had faced three-
on-one fights in his line of work. Not often, of course, but he
had. And right now he had Chicken on his side. Three-on-
two was far more commonplace. Nothing special about that,
save for the fact that this time zombies comprised the majority
of the opposing force.

"Chicken," he said.

"Y-yes?" she replied.

"Can you see where Rabbit is right now? With your ability?"

"O-of course," she said, pride edging into her voice, stam-
mer or no. "I've been keeping track of him. I'm keeping my
watchers a fair distance away so that Rabbit won't realize he's
being watched, but the birds have made following him, Boar,
and Snake their top priority."

"All right. Listen, I hate working with others, but just in
this case, I'll make an exception for you. I accept your offer."

In not so many words, I'm doing you a favor—and I'm the
one in charge.

Whether or not she got the subtext, she broke into a huge
grin and said, "And—and Rabbit?"

"We're going rabbit hunting. We'll kill him."

"All right! Yeah!" Chicken said, complete with a fist pump.
"We can do this! We're gonna make it all the way to the end!"

Dog didn't intend for their alliance to go that far. He only
meant to work together until they'd defeated Rabbit, or maybe

just a little while after. Of course, he didn't say as much.

"Well then," Chicken said, offering an innocent hand-shake. "Let me introduce myself."

"I am Niwatori, the Fighter of the Chicken. I kill by pecks."

"I am Dokku, the Fighter of the Dog. I kill in bites."

Now, just how can I use her?

As he met her slender hand with his, Dog's mind went to work on that cruel calculation—of when the drawbacks of having her around would outweigh the usefulness of keeping her alive.

4

As the two pursued Team Rabbit, Dog decided to exchange information with Chicken. Of the Zodiac War's twelve combatants, roughly half were unknown to him. Information was as much a part of this battle as anything, and as an alliance, sharing what they knew was important. Besides, Dog wanted to gain Chicken's trust, and to do that, he needed to act as if he'd actually bought in to this partnership. Anyway, it had to be more interesting than the small talk she had been offering.

"You know that song 'Furusato,' right?" started one nugget. "How it starts out with the lyrics 'the mountain where I chased rabbits, the river where I fished small carp,' and people often mishear it as, 'the mountain where there's tasty rabbits'? Well, if the person in the song was catching carp, if you really think about it, sooner or later they probably did eat those rabbits too. And I bet they *were* tasty."

Maybe this was just her way of building his trust.

"I know five of the fighters," Dog offered. "Ox, Dragon, Snake, Monkey, and Boar." This was the truth. He saw no problem in giving real information to someone he was going to kill regardless. After all, she might feel obligated to give him information in return that could be invaluable. "The most dangerous is Ox. How can I put it?" Dog thought for a second. "He's incomprehensibly strong. No one has ever stood on a battlefield against him and survived to tell about it. People call him the Natural-Born Slayer."

"The Natural-Born…Slayer?"

"That's right. He's a top competitor, no doubt about it. You'd have to be as good in a fight as me to take him on unprepared. If you stumble across him, I suggest you run."

"Okay," Chicken said, though she didn't seem to grasp the severity of the threat.

No matter. You'll be dead by my hand before you get the chance to run into Ox.

Dog continued, "As for the Tatsumi Brothers—that's Dragon and Snake—there's nothing to say about them. The twins made for a hell of a team together, but one is already dead, and either's not half as tough on his own."

"I see."

"Now, Monkey… Well, you saw who she is. She's a pacifist—a real bleeding heart. I can't stand her myself. A disgrace of a warrior, if you ask me. She makes her living going into war zones and mediating the disputes. Her peace treaties have brought many a war to its ceasefire."

That's going to be your downfall too, Dog thought. *You shouldn't have attempted to sign on to Team Monkey, and you really shouldn't have come to me.*

"To us mercs," Dog said, "she's bad for business. I wouldn't be surprised if she's participating in the Zodiac War because she thinks she can end it."

"Do you think she can?"

Dog didn't answer. It seemed impossible, but some small part of him feared she could, and another almost hoped she would.

"I don't think we need to talk about Boar," Dog said. "She's just Rabbit's slave now. She could do this thing with her guns she called 'Making It Rain' that you wouldn't want to be on the wrong side of. You could even say it's lucky for us that she died so early." Then he asked, "So, Niwatori, who do you know?"

"Oh, I, ah, don't know much about anyone. Just rumors I wouldn't trust. I'm sorry. I-I wish I could be more helpful."

This was a bit of a letdown, but Dog hadn't expected much from her anyway.

He wasn't feeling particularly crestfallen, but then Chicken added, as if just remembering, "Oh! But, Dokku-san, don't you wonder about that boy?"

"Who do you mean, that boy?"

"The sleepy one. You know, that one who kept dozing off? He didn't seem like the fighting type." She paused, then said, "I don't think he could be much older than fifteen, do you?"

Dog wasn't sure Chicken was in any position to say anyone else didn't seem like much of a fighter, but she wasn't wrong. That kid seemed out of place among the fighters, like Rabbit had with his bloody blade, only in a much different way.

Dog asked, "Do you think we need to be wary of him?"

"No, it's not that I think he's tough or something like that. It's just—I feel like I've seen him before. In some other context. Do you get that feeling?"

Now that she mentioned it, he did have the vague sense of having seen the kid before. But he didn't know where. Had they shared a battlefield? Had they been allies or opponents?

"Oh!" Chicken exclaimed. Dog turned to her and noticed a sparrow perched on her shoulder. "Oh, Dokku-san, this is bad. Rabbit's team has split in two!"

5

When Dog heard that Rabbit's team had split into two, he assumed that meant that Rabbit, in essence their commanding officer, had sent the two reanimated corpses off on their own. Instead, it was Boar—the woman with the twin machine guns—who had peeled off from the other two. With blood oozing from the gash in her chest made by Rabbit's giant blade, Boar roamed the empty city, her eyes as lifeless as the ghost town streets. Gone was any sign of nobility in her shambling gait, no trace of her in there anywhere at all. She was, in every sense, a walking dead. This wasn't some high-class lady out for a stroll, but an eerie monster on the prowl.

"I'm sorry," Chicken said. "I lost Rabbit and Snake. I think he might have realized he was being followed."

She sounded embarrassed, but as far as Dog was concerned, she'd already done more than could be expected of such an inexperienced fighter. But if Rabbit had figured out that the birds were watching him, why would he send Boar off on her own like that? Why wouldn't he try to hide her—or at least hide the fact she was undead?

Is this a trap?

Maybe Rabbit was using the unsteady and feeble-looking woman as bait to draw out other fighters whom he and Snake would then ambush from behind. All warriors, no matter how skilled, were at their most vulnerable when already in a fight. No matter how bizarre Rabbit might act, judging from the way Chicken described his takedown of Boar, the man was not crazy.

Well, to use his own ally as bait requires a certain kind of crazy.

The mad dog would have to be willing to go even further if he wanted to overcome this adversary.

"Niwatori," he said.

"Y-yes? What is it?" Chicken asked.

"Give me your arm."

"Like this?" she said uneasily, but she offered her arm.

Without another word, Dog bit, sinking his teeth into her flesh.

She gave a startled shriek, but the anesthetic coating on his fangs should have numbed any pain. The procedure was over in less than a second. Dog released her arm and said, "How do you feel?"

"How-how do I feel? I don't even know what you did to me."

"Just a little performance enhancement."

When Dog bit his targets, his poison produced many effects ranging from death to more death—but not necessarily limited to death. Not all toxins had to be deadly. Some could be used for doping.

This one Dog called the "One-Man Army." The drug drew out its user's latent potential, but it was strong stuff and could push a body too far. For that reason, Dog would never consider subjecting himself to its effects. But it would give Chicken a boost—for a time, at least.

His plan was this: he would send out the powered-up Chicken to face Boar—the bait—alone. It didn't matter who won; he just needed Chicken to put up a decent fight. What was important was for Rabbit and Snake to reveal themselves. Then, Dog would ambush them. When Dog sank his teeth into Rabbit, they would not be filled with doping drugs, but lethal poison. It would mean certain death for Rabbit. Doping or not, Chicken would surely be killed by one of their three opponents, but that would only make things easier for Dog in the end.

Then, fresh from the hunt, I'll return to hiding.

While Dog was lost in such sinister thoughts, a confused Chicken was swinging her arm, testing its inexplicable, new-found strength. "W-what is this?" she said. "What is this?"

"Stay calm," Dog said. "All I did was unlock power you already possessed. Steady yourself. Control it."

"C-control it," Chicken said in that same nervous, rushed voice as before. "You mean, like this?"

Those were the last words Dog would ever hear.

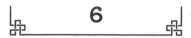

6

Having crushed open Dog's head with her bare hands, Chicken let out a deep sigh and said, "I can't believe that took so long. But it's done now. I finally got that boost."

She plunged her hand into his now-exposed neck cavity and found the poison jewel, as good as new. "Dokku-san, I know I *told* you I didn't know anything about the others, but actually, I knew about you."

She knew he led others to believe that biting was his fighting technique when in fact he was a master poisoner, and she even knew about his most secret concoction, the One-Man Army. Dog believed he had kept his secrets hidden, but he was wrong to think he could hide anything from her Eye of the Cormorant.

Going into this battle, Chicken was well aware she lacked strength and experience. That was why she spared no effort in digging up as much information as she could on every fighter who had a chance of participating in the Zodiac War. She hadn't made first contact with Dog by mere chance—she had him in her sights from the start. And now that he'd fulfilled his role in her plan, she killed him.

One reason for her betrayal was that she didn't want to risk him bestowing the One-Man Army, or some similar boon, on any other fighter. But at her core Chicken just didn't trust anyone else—she might need to use someone from time to time, but never would she consider actually teaming up with another person. When she'd raised her hand to ally with Monkey, she'd done so with a heart full of betrayal.

All the way to his end, Dog had perceived her timidity as nothing more than that. But timidity didn't always equal weakness. For Chicken, it was something closer to strength; fear gave her the determination to take any action necessary in the name of self-preservation.

That didn't mean she was without gratitude. She bowed her head in respect to her fellow fighter and spoke—although he was in no condition to reply. "Thank you, Dokku. Because of what you've done, there's now a chance I can win this. If I do, I'll erect a statue in your honor. I promise you."

She had already forgotten what his face used to look like, but men weren't really about their faces, were they? As long as the statue had fangs like his, that should be good enough.

Now that that was over with, she turned her attention to the roaming, machine-gun-wielding corpse. "On to the next one. Here I come!"

CHICKEN VS. ~~DOG~~
END OF THE 2ND BATTLE

THE THIRD BATTLE

"Using an ox-cleaver to cut up fowl."

**NIWATORI,
THE FIGHTER OF
THE CHICKEN**

"I wish for myself."

REAL NAME: Ryōka NIWA
BORN: June 6
HEIGHT: 153 cm
WEIGHT: 42 kg

Throughout her early childhood, Ryōka was the victim of abuse so abhorrent that words fail to describe it. She has no memories of her youth before the age of fifteen—she doesn't know what happened, what was done to her, or what she had done. Her first memory is that of standing over a pulpy mess that seemed to have once been her parents, with a warm and bloody egg slicer in her hand. The authorities took her into their care, but the Niwa family took notice of her abilities and, after adopting her, began to force her to fight for them. Given no clear purpose, volition, or convictions of her own, she had only her orders. Because she has no qualms about killing or perpetrating deception or betrayal, her role on the battlefield is often that of the spy. But after years of duplicity, she is beginning to find it hard to tell friend from foe.

Her weapon is not a trident but rather a spading fork, which she has taken to calling Cockscomb. When she feels overstressed, she likes to go to an *onsen*, and she's always a little bit happier when her battles take her near a spa resort. Her favorite food is eggs slow-cooked in the hot spring water.

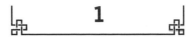

1

Timid, but not weak; not strong, but determined. Not powerful, but not powerless; not hyperintelligent, but cunning. Niwatori, the Fighter of the Chicken, approached fighting now much as she had the first time she took up arms. She never cared at all about whatever gap in skill or ability might exist between her and her opponents, nor did she factor in their unique qualities or character traits. She could respect and appreciate her more formidable enemies, but ultimately, such things were situational—as mutable as the weather. The very best fighter might have an off day, and the weakest might hit upon a lucky break. The virtuous could be corrupted, and evildoers could reform. Such vagaries never captured her attention.

It's myself I need to be thinking of.

She wasn't self-indulgent or needlessly violent, but rather the opposite—she was so meek and restrained as to border on servile. But few were as self-possessed as she. To Chicken, other people were merely background elements. The Zodiac War's principal rule—victory goes to the last survivor—suited her surprisingly well.

Of all twelve warriors participating in this contest—an event that came only once every twelve years with the promise of fulfilling any single wish—perhaps she alone viewed it not as a spectacle, but as a simple extension of her normal way of life.

When it came to Rabbit's plan to use Boar's corpse as live bait—or at least, undead bait—Chicken might not have grasped the necromanticist's strategy as thoroughly as Dog had, but like Dog, she wasn't distracted by the repulsive nature of Rabbit's tactics. She found the man disturbing and creepy, of that there was no doubt, but that too was simply circumstance. And it was one she had turned to her own benefit.

By revealing what she knew about Rabbit, she was able to instill fear in Dog, lure him from his place of hiding, and at last, entice him into injecting his One-Man Army drug into her. Perils weren't to be managed; they were to be leveraged. Chicken trusted nothing but her own abilities, and for a time, they had been boosted to their limit. Now she wanted to put an end to this contest before the effects wore off.

But this rush of power wasn't going to tempt her into attacking Boar's shambling corpse. Chicken wasn't so reckless as to rush headlong into a field test before getting better acquainted with her new strength—at least, not when she had a better way, a way in which she could take care of Boar from afar.

In dealing with Dog, Chicken had perhaps oversold the threat posed by Rabbit's undead soldiers. Though the necromanticist was indeed a threat to her, he wasn't anything she couldn't handle.

Wielding her spading fork, Cockscomb, like an orchestra conductor's baton, she flicked her wrist, and for a moment, nothing seemed to change. But several seconds later, the effects were dramatic. A roar of hundreds of flapping wings cracked through the air above Boar's walking corpse and announced the descent of the birds themselves, a torrential downpour of sparrows, swallows, crows, doves, skylarks, black kites, hawks, hummingbirds, and cuckoos alike and more, all acting as one.

As Chicken watched, she announced, "I kill by pecks," though her target was too far, and maybe too dead, to hear. Every bird in the vicinity of the abandoned city had gathered to peck at Boar's corpse. "I give to you my Sky Burial."

Dog's secret power was the One-Man Army, and this was Chicken's—although she typically used it to clean up the battlefield after all the fighting was done. Unlike a video game, in the real world your enemies didn't simply disappear after hitting the ground. It was a dilemma that had plagued soldiers of all stripes across the ages. But not Chicken.

There was an old saying, "A bird does not foul the nest it's about to leave." In other words, a person should leave a place the way they found it. After her battles were won, Chicken instructed her birds to consume the bodies. Paired with her Eye of the Cormorant, the two abilities constituted a mutually beneficial relationship between her and the birds. She would provide them with regular meals, and they would provide her with information. She had only kept her so-called Sky Burial a secret because she didn't ever want to be forced to use it to clean up after other people's messes.

Chicken was never the best strategist, but the advantage the Sky Burial provided her against Rabbit was so overwhelming that even she had no trouble grasping it. Normally, she would have trouble convincing the birds to attack a living adversary—such an act was beyond the scope of their arrangement—but Rabbit's allies were corpses. Moreover, the undead were an affront to nature.

In one moment, hundreds of birds stripped Boar's corpse to the bones, and in the next moment, even the bones had been carried away—probably to serve as nest-building material. But even though it was a corpse, it was an animated corpse—specifically, the animated corpse of a warrior chosen for the Zodiac War. The birds, though many, were merely birds, and the undead fighter hadn't gone down without resistance. A few dozen dead birds had been left behind, their bodies scattered nearby. Apparently, Boar had managed to shoot them down, though the sound of her gunfire was drowned out by the flapping of the swarm. Now those guns, too, had fallen to the empty street.

What had she called her ability—"Making It Rain"?

Chicken hadn't needed to be told that by Dog. Her birds had already told her before he had the chance. Boar was capable of spraying those two machine guns without ever needing to stop to reload, and judging by the number of birds she had shot down, her corpse had still been in command of that power.

Chicken had assumed that once dead, the fighters' skills would be lost to them. Lucky for her, she hadn't let her own enhanced strength get to her head. Had she instead decided to test herself directly against Boar, she would likely be covered from head to toe with bullet holes. Chicken's faulty assumption nearly cost her life.

Even this was costly. The birds were too few before, and now they're even fewer.

Ideally, she would have had enough birds at her call to watch over every opponent and provide her with complete awareness of the battlefield. But that was the world of the ideal. What she had was reality. The ghost city had, by definition, been a city. That meant fewer birds and far fewer species compared to more rural areas. She'd expended a significant number of those, and reinforcements were limited.

Chicken didn't feel any particular love for her birds; nor was she particularly sad that some had given their lives in sacrifice to protect hers. But she didn't like losing them. She also didn't like that the departing survivors hadn't lifted a finger—or a beak, rather—to the carcasses of their compatriots, which they had simply left behind. She'd never known those ravenous creatures to leave any table scraps.

They must be full, Chicken thought.

Even if she happened across Snake's walking corpse, she wouldn't be able to summon another Sky Burial. At least not until she gave the birds a little time to digest.

I'd better back off for the time being. I'll put the birds back on recon duty.

And so Chicken set out to put some space between her and the other fighters. For now, she was content that she had disposed of one corpse.

2

Even though Chicken didn't think deeply on her decision to dispose of Boar's corpse, she resisted the lure of a bolder move—for example, tracking Boar until the roaming corpse rejoined Rabbit and Snake and attempting to take out all three in one fell swoop—and instead made a small, but real, change to the course of the Zodiac War. The necromanticist's ability to forge an unbreakable alliance posed as significant a threat as Dog had suspected. If let be, Rabbit would bring the battle to a swift and decisive conclusion. But just as his alliance was getting off the ground, Chicken put the brakes on it—and that was a major accomplishment.

No matter how dangerous a fighter Rabbit was, with only Snake at his command, he was not in a position to make any big moves. The ambush that had worked so effectively against Boar would not be easily replicated—the only reason he was able to take Boar by complete surprise was the location of their stand-off, right where the battle had started, where Snake's dead body was both nearby and entirely inconspicuous. Now Rabbit would have no choice but to adopt a more reactive stance.

The actions of the clever, duplicitous Team Chicken and Dog had succeeded in bringing the Zodiac War into a deadlock, and the fighter in the best position to capitalize on this stalemate was none other than Chicken. No matter how limited the number of her flock, given enough time, the birds would reveal her opponents wherever their hiding places might be.

Chicken only faced one problem—she didn't realize the extent of her advantage. She was used to fighting from a position of weakness and inexperience and making an unfavorable position work to her benefit. Actually having the advantage was decidedly unfamiliar to her. Were she to grasp the nature of the position she now held, she would surely put it to good use. But before she had that chance, a voice called out to her.

"Hey, lady," the voice said.

Chicken was inside a convenience store far away from the street where Boar had received her burial-of-sorts. Watching the birds feed hadn't exactly been appetizing, but nevertheless, Chicken sought to fortify herself with a meal as well. Some fighters were of the opinion that taking time to eat during a battle was imprudent at best, but Chicken was not one for fighting on an empty stomach. Fortunately for her, the coolers' contents had been left behind, and she was just taking her pick from the various drinks and prepared foods when the voice spoke.

She turned and saw the teenaged boy who had been half—or maybe even fully—asleep through much of the opening assembly.

With a startled cry, Chicken scooped up Cockscomb and pointed its three tips at her opponent. He was just a boy, delicate and not so well built. In her powered-up state, could Chicken take him in close combat? Should she summon her birds to at least give her more vantage points?

"Ahh, give it a rest," he said, as listlessly as before. "I don't mean to fight you." He raised his hands in the universal gesture of surrender. But Chicken knew better than to trust that for more than it was worth.

She asked, "H-how did you know to find me here?"

"I didn't. I just came here to find some food, same as you."

If Chicken had understood the advantage she held in the battle, she might have held off on her meal and done more to solidify her position, and she might not have so incautiously gone into this convenience store. If what the boy said was true, and this was mere coincidence, then it was still a coincidence her carelessness had brought upon her.

As Chicken nursed her embarrassment at having put herself in this entirely avoidable situation, the boy said, "Well, I might as well introduce myself.

"I am Nezumi, the Fighter of the Rat. I kill inexorably."

Chicken hadn't expected him to have the proper manners to give the customary introduction. Of course, she hadn't expected him at all—which was why, too caught by surprise, she failed to respond with hers in turn.

So he's Rat...

She had heard that his was an exceedingly peculiar clan, but her Eye of the Cormorant hadn't ever been able to find out anything about him.

"And you are?" the boy asked.

"Oh, er, I'm Niwatori, the Fighter of the Chicken," she said somewhat vacuously, but better late than never. "I kill by pecks."

"Uh-huh," Rat said, giving her the once-over with those sleepy eyes and going to no lengths to hide it. "Oh, that's right, you raised your hand back there, didn't you?"

"Back where? Oh. Yes, I did." Chicken had almost forgotten. "With Monkey, yes. What about it?"

She had volunteered to join Monkey, albeit with the full intention of betraying her. Rat raised his hand too—first, in fact, which had made it easier for Chicken to follow.

"W-why do you ask?" Chicken said.

"Come with me," Rat replied. "I'll take you to where Monkey is."

3

Rat took her back underground. This time, it wasn't any car park where a bird might enter, should it be struck by the inclination, but a place where entrance required lifting a manhole cover. The sewer was perhaps the most obvious of hiding places, but with the entire city abandoned, far more savory shelters abounded, and few would think to seek out any quarry here. At the very least, it would likely have remained in Chicken's blind spot had she not been ushered here like this. Even now, Chicken was having trouble believing anyone would put up with the lack of electricity and that god-awful stench to set up base here for a long stretch.

"Ah, Nezumi-kun, you're back," Monkey said. Chicken had suspected that Monkey wouldn't actually be here, but here she was. "Did you find any food?" Then, noticing Chicken, she said, "Oh, who did you bring?"

Monkey was sitting on a spread-out blanket as if she were having a picnic. She emanated such a lively and carefree aura that Chicken almost forgot they were in a sewer, let alone in the middle of a contest to the death.

"Yeah, I found food," Rat said. "She was there, so I brought her."

His answer explained so little he might as well have not said anything at all. Chicken felt put on the spot.

If you're going to force someone to come all the way to a place like this, she thought, *you could at least not leave her hanging.*

Not that Rat had forced her there at all. In fact, Rat had simply started walking and said hardly a word the entire way. If anything, it felt like Chicken had just decided to tag along.

And he just kept his back to me the whole time. He left himself wide open.

Even without Dog's One-Man Army—even if Chicken were her normal, unenhanced self—she could have run him through with her fork without any trouble. Watching him from behind, he seemed every bit the plain teenager with nothing of the warrior in him at all, just as he'd come across on the observation deck. It was almost harder *not* to kill him.

But...maybe that's why I followed him so blindly. If I sensed any fight in him, I might have killed him instead. I didn't kill him simply because he was so killable. If I could do it anytime I wanted, why do it now?

Compared to Dog, who left so few openings for an attack that when he let his guard down for a single moment, she felt she had no choice but to kill him, maybe Rat did have, in his own way, some aptitude for survival. Meanwhile, as Chicken was attempting to give the boy some sort of charitable benefit of the doubt, Rat simply laid himself down on the blanket, where he folded his arms beneath his head, crossed his legs, and closed his eyes.

"Come now, Nezumi," Monkey said, scolding him.

But Rat drowsily replied, "I'm tired from going out. So I'm sleeping. You take it from here." He didn't say anything else and seemed to already be asleep.

Some people said that one proof of a warrior was the ability to get in some sleep whenever and wherever the moment presented itself. Chicken saw truth in that idea, but she doubted it meant falling asleep in total indifference to the ongoing fight.

I thought maybe we'd met before, but talking to him hasn't stirred up many memories. Maybe that feeling I had was just a trick of my imagination.

"Sometimes," Monkey said with an exasperated sigh, "I don't know what to do with this boy." She shifted herself to face Chicken. "Sorry about that. Really, he's not a bad kid. He's just…"

"Ah, oh," Chicken stammered. "It's fine. Don't worry about it."

"You raised your hand for me in the tower, didn't you? Do you know who I am?"

"I know you're the Fighter of the Monkey, but that's all."

Unlike in her dealings with Dog, Chicken was telling the truth this time. Monkey's clan, as with Rat's, was shrouded in mystery that not even her Eye of the Cormorant had been able to penetrate. Brusque Rat and affable Monkey were vastly different personalities, but to Chicken, they both presented unsettling and unfamiliar fighters. As such, they required her caution—but caution alone wouldn't get her anywhere. She was timid but not weak; she was not strong, but she was determined.

"I see," Monkey said with the kind of smile you wouldn't give to an enemy you were about to face in mortal combat. "Then let me introduce myself.

"I am Sharyū, the Fighter of the Monkey. I kill in peace."

"I am Niwatori, the Fighter of the Chicken. I kill by pecks."

This time, Chicken responded straightaway. And when

Monkey said "in peace," the words rang true. Maybe that ceasefire the woman proposed at the very beginning wasn't, as Chicken had suspected, simply a means to forming an alliance. Maybe Monkey actually intended to end the Zodiac War without any death.

No, that can't be, Chicken thought, pushing away any such distracting thoughts. *Dokku seemed to have that same misconception. Nobody would seriously consider cooperating with their opponents to attempt to bypass the Zodiac War.*

"Well, Niwatori-san, it's nice to meet you." Monkey's words carried no trace of deception—only friendship. "I appreciate your stepping forward back there, and I'm glad that we're able to have a real talk now."

"Yeah, okay."

"After we all got split up, I managed to find Nezumi," Monkey said, glancing at the sleeping youth. "He suggested we hide down here."

That made sense. After all, sewers have long been passages for rodents.

Monkey continued, "After the floor fell out, I wasn't sure I'd ever be able to meet up with the people who so kindly volunteered to join me, but this is a good start."

"Ah, yes," Chicken replied, omitting the fact that she had only raised her hand because she thought betraying the woman would put her in a good position. "Yeah, I'm, uh…glad I came."

This wasn't like when she found Dog in the underground garage. His intention to use and then kill her had been blatantly obvious. Monkey was different. She seemed utterly devoid of that maliciousness everyone else carried somewhere inside them. Chicken found herself believing that Monkey was truly, from the bottom of her heart, happy to see her.

The question is, can I kill her?

If Monkey was really a kind person, and if she really hoped for peace, then to Chicken, she was easy to kill. She wouldn't have to put on the buffoon act to get Monkey's guard down as had been required with Dog. She could just kill Monkey without any of that trouble. Sure, with Rat there, it was two against one, but they were nothing Chicken couldn't handle, now that she was operating at maximum power.

But here, as before, this position—having the freedom to kill them whenever she wanted—kept her in a state of inaction. In every battle, she had fought under the motto "Kill the enemies you can kill, when you can kill them." She was just unaccustomed to fighting from a position of strength.

But that wasn't even the real issue. What she was truly unaccustomed to was dealing with someone who, like Monkey, had no hidden side. Neither on nor off the battlefield had she ever encountered such a person.

Monkey said, "I just wish there was a way we could join back up with everyone who raised their hands."

Chicken didn't know how to respond. Was this woman seriously still trying to find a surefire way to win the Zodiac War without anyone fighting or getting hurt, even now that the battle was already underway?

Chicken tried to recall who had raised their hand. Aside from Monkey, Rat, and herself, there were three others. Ox, Horse—the giant one—and Rabbit.

Surely she won't include Rabbit. He was clearly just trying to stir up chaos. This woman isn't that much of a saint. Hell, even I can see how stupid that would be.

Not to mention that Chicken wasn't genuinely on board when she raised her hand. Ox and Horse were suspect too. She couldn't even be sure of the sleeping Rat's true intentions. Even if Monkey was serious, whatever hopes she had for ending the Zodiac War without violence and death was nothing more than a pipe dream. It would never happen.

Monkey was saying, "Have you seen anyone else? What's going on aboveground?"

"Some are already dead." Chicken didn't need to be so blunt about it, but some malicious part of her hoped to smash that woman's earnest idealism. "I know for a fact that Boar and Dog have been killed. Including Snake, that makes at least three out. That's a quarter of us already gone."

Chicken of course didn't mention that she was the one who had killed Dog. She had washed her hands and cleaned off any telltale blood splatters from her clothes. The sole reason she wore such skimpy clothing was to make the blood easier to wash off.

Chicken asked, "Even with three dead, can your plan still work?"

"It can. But it's still too soon to reveal the details, I'm afraid." Then, with real disappointment in her voice, Monkey said, "So two more have died. That's too bad." She made no effort to hide the fact that this news came as a surprise; nor did she try to act like it didn't disturb her. "That means we may see more victims yet. All right, I can't afford inaction any longer. It's time to do something…possibly as soon as after we eat. Niwatori, you'll dine with us, won't you?"

It was an innocent invitation, delivered as if there was no imaginable reason Chicken would refuse. Chicken only had one moment to decide. To accept or to kill?

She decided.

4

Five minutes later, Chicken was back aboveground. She had politely declined Monkey's invitation and bade both her and Rat farewell—though the teenager had remained asleep through the entire exchange, so in truth, she had only really engaged with Monkey.

What the hell is wrong with me? Chicken asked herself. *How stupid am I? I could have at least pretended to go along with her.* Instead, she had declined not only the meal, but the alliance. *Where's that determined, crafty person I used to be?* How she would have played it was obvious: pretend to be their ally, get close to them, and take Cockscomb in hand and skewer that trusting, chatty Monkey and the sleepy boy then and there. It was as if she had been poisoned by Monkey's pacifism—like those clear, unsuspecting eyes had pierced right through her.

Chicken could still hear Monkey's voice, disappointed but still friendly, and it ached in her chest.

"Oh, that's unfortunate," Monkey had said. "If you change your mind, you're welcome to return anytime. I'll be here, waiting. Please don't lose hope."

It's probably the fault of that One-Man Army stuff. That potion enhanced my mind along with my body. It made my stupid head smarter. Because I went off and gave myself this boost, I lost who I really am. That's why I let myself become torn apart by some bogus notion of kindness and sincerity. What a fool I am. What good is this strength if it makes me too uncertain to act?

Whether her analysis was true or not was a mystery that would never find an answer. The theory wasn't far-fetched. The toxic drug that coursed through her might very well have caused a resurgence in her normally suppressed nervous streak, taking away her usual determined self. But before she had the opportunity to examine her theory in detail, she stumbled across another fighter.

This encounter, as before, would have been avoidable had she been using her birds to keep watch from above.

"Are you alone?" the man asked.

With a little startled jump, Chicken turned to see who it was. Just her luck. Of all twelve fighters, it had to be the most famous. Of all twelve, it had to be the most renowned. Of all twelve, it had to be Ox. When Chicken was with Dog, she had feigned ignorance, but of course, she knew about this man. Any soldier whose feet have touched a battlefield wouldn't need Eye of the Cormorant to know who he was.

But no one really knows how strong he is—because none have faced the Natural-Born Slayer and lived.

"I don't suppose you'll answer me, will you?" Ox was saying. "If there was anyone with you, I'd just like to know is all. Doesn't really matter to me if there's more of you or not."

The saber he casually held, along with his matador garb, were coated red with blood—and enough of it to clearly not be his own. He hadn't tried to hide it. While Chicken, despite having boosted her abilities to their absolute limits, had wiped herself clean of Dog's blood and had made every effort to remove any trace she had been in a battle, Ox's appearance announced without reservation: "I don't need to hide or change who I am."

And, Chicken thought, *if he has someone else's blood splattered all over him, that means he's already been in battle.* If the rumors—the legends—were real, whoever that person was, they were surely dead.

Chicken said, "I-I thought you were a pacifist."

"No, I think that's just Monkey. Sure, I volunteered to join her, but I was just looking for a team. Once we all got scattered, there was no point. That peace treaty was dead in the water." Ox seemed to realize something. "Wait, what made you bring her up all of a sudden? Is she nearby?"

He was quick-witted—no enhancement drug needed there. Chicken gasped and raised Cockscomb, pointing its three tips toward him.

"Well, well," Ox said, "I didn't figure you for that type. You're thinking about fighting me to protect Monkey, is that it? 'If you want to pass, you'll have to defeat me first,' eh? I suggest you reconsider. That's not the kind of motivation that will make you fight well. It's not right for you. Someone else, maybe. But you're the kind of person who needs to fight for herself."

Ox seemed to be stating his thoughts as they came to him, and Chicken found herself in complete agreement. But then she was announcing herself.

"I am Niwatori, the Fighter of the Chicken. I kill by pecks."

"I am Ushii, the Fighter of the Ox. I just kill."

It was over in the blink of an eye. Actually, it happened faster than that. In less time than it took an eye to close, Ox's two saber thrusts pierced through Chicken's eyes so fast as to be near simultaneous.

Neither Chicken's enhanced abilities nor her uncharacter-istic motivation was of any use in the face of pure strength. She had been the same as dead the moment she had come face to face with Ox.

He's so incomprehensibly powerful.

She had been defeated by a natural warrior—one who did not need to rely on skill, strategy, deception, bargaining, transformation, enhancement, or most of all, circumstance. A strong will meant nothing in the face of true strength.

So…this is all I could be.

Chicken certainly felt no satisfaction in dying a somewhat noble death. But to die without pain or suffering, by the well-honed edge of an expert swordsman's blade, might have been the best thing that had ever happened to her.

Thank you for everything, my birds, Chicken thought just before the end. *You must be getting hungry again. Come, eat your fill.*

OX VS. ~~CHICKEN~~
END OF THE 3ᴿᴰ BATTLE

THE FOURTH BATTLE

"Even among one's formidable enemies,
some are monkeys that scratch and claw."

SHARYŪ,
THE FIGHTER OF
THE MONKEY

"I wish for peace."

REAL NAME: Misaki YŪKI
BORN: July 7
HEIGHT: 150 cm
WEIGHT: 40 kg

She was given life on a sacred mountain, where three mountain hermits—Mizaru, the Unseeing Water Monkey; Iwazaru, the Unspeaking Rock Monkey; and Kikazaru, the Unhearing Vapor Monkey—taught her the fundamentals of combat. With the aid of her mountain magic, which gives her the power to manipulate liquids, solids, and gases, she has the potential for being an incredibly superior warrior, but she has never used her mystical techniques to harm another person. As a pacifist and a warrior, she has chosen a life of contradiction, and through her actions she has brought peaceful resolution to 314 wars and 229 internal conflicts.

Rather than traditional weapons, she wields ceasefire negotiations and peace treaty proposals. Because her feats aren't as easily recognized as simply killing her enemies would be, she remains markedly unknown as a fighter. But those few who know of her consider her a hero beyond compare.

Her private life is one of normalcy. She makes pastries as a hobby, and the desserts she creates are so delicious they often tempt her into overeating. She lives with her boyfriend of five years and is starting to think about marriage.

1

Rat, apparently awake now, said without any other lead-in, "That flighty lady—I think she's probably dead by now."

Sharyū, the Fighter of the Monkey, put down her meal and calmly asked, "Why do you think that? Is your special ability being able to sense such things?"

Rat was still sleepily sprawled on the blanket. "I'd hardly call it a special ability," he said. "Her fate is plain enough for anyone to see. Although, well, you know—rats have a knack for fleeing ships that are about to sink. Maybe some people have the shadow of death over them, and I can just see it better than others."

Monkey said nothing. His emotions remained masked to her. If she had to say she saw some feeling in him, it was that he wanted to go back to sleep and nothing more.

The boy continued, "But if that lady is dead, it's your fault, Miss Sharyū."

She paused. "And why do you think that?"

"She didn't look all that tough, but she was still a warrior. The people running this thing wouldn't have put her in if she didn't have a decent shot at surviving. But the more she talked with you, the weaker she got. She went from fainthearted to just plain faint. Your goodwill changed something in her. You reformed her. Who she was at the end…even a civvie could have killed her. To a rogue like her, your lack of venom is itself a deadly poison."

Just how long has this boy been awake? Monkey wondered. *I thought he was asleep the whole time.* She and the child had stuck together since almost the very start of the Zodiac War, but he rarely spoke. He had not opened up to her, and he kept his opinions to himself—until now. *What's caused this change of heart? Or is this a change at all?*

"Listen, Nezumi," she said. "Are you...are you trying to provoke me? I'm sorry, but I can be a little slow to pick up on such things."

"Is that so?" the child said. "Well, I'll say no more. Even if I can read someone's fate, I can't read their mind. Anyway, whatever else happens, you won't be reforming me. So you don't have to worry about that."

Monkey still couldn't see what he was getting at. She was glad he was speaking to her now at least, but if all they did was talk past each other, it would be no more fruitful than idle chatter.

Rat asked, "But where does that leave your plan? Assuming that lady is in fact dead, that means that four of us have been killed. And that's only the ones we know of. That's a full third gone. Can you still pull off this guaranteed plan for victory of yours?"

"I can, although I'm saddened that fewer people remain to be saved. It sounds like you're operating under a mistaken assumption, so allow me to correct it. I don't have just one plan."

That startled Rat a little. "You've got more than one?"

"I'm not so carelessly optimistic as to believe I can stop the Zodiac War with just one plan. Treaties always require flexibility in order to adapt to changing circumstances."

Rat nodded with a thoughtful hum. "Well, I've never really thought much about stopping the fight, so I'll leave that part to you."

"Say, Nezumi," Monkey said.

"What?"

"First you say I'm not going to reform you, and now you say you don't care about stopping this war. If you have no enthusiasm for my plans, then why did you agree to join me? I don't figure you for a pacifist either."

Monkey had tossed her remark out there to make Rat think, never expecting he'd answer, but some part of it drew out a frank reply.

"You want to know what I think about peace? Actually, I hate it," the boy said. "When I'm not out on some battlefield, in my so called normal life, I'm in high school. My classmates—peace has made them all go soft. Damn wastes, all of them. The thought of risking my life to protect their meaningless existences is revolting."

Monkey said nothing.

Rat continued, "Doesn't it bother you? No one in the world has saved as many lives as you have. But a decent number of those you've saved are garbage—that's just plain math. Actually, what you do is even worse. By saving people, you're turning them into garbage. They think of wars and killing as someone else's job. They think that people like me fight because that's what we want to do. I hate to say it, but the more I protect them, the more I just want to kill them."

Monkey let him continue.

"So tell me, Miss Pacifist. How the hell do you come to terms with that feeling?"

These feelings were a product of his age, but Monkey sensed they deserved to be handled with care. The easy response would have been to dismiss such emotions as childish and to say that he would understand when he grew up. But plenty of people reached adulthood still carrying thoughts like that. The best Monkey could do was to give him an honest and direct answer.

"I don't make peace with it," she said. "I struggle with it my whole life."

"Ah, I see. The perfect answer from a saint. But talk like that doesn't reach us mere mortals."

Finally, Rat sat up. Despite the child's claims, her words seemed to have roused something in his stubborn heart—or at least, they roused his upper body from the floor.

"So," Rat said, "are you like a hard case or something?"

"Well, I know some self-defense tactics. I couldn't survive on the battlefield if I didn't."

"Come on, you can drop the modesty. After all, you're the one who blasted the floor apart, aren't you?"

So he knew. There really was more to this boy than appearances suggested.

"I wasn't trying to hide that I did it," Monkey said, but then stopped herself. "No, I suppose I was trying to hide it. I didn't want you looking at me like you are now."

"I'm not being critical," Rat said. "I've always had this look on my face. Was born with it. I don't mean anything, really. Anyway, you only did it because you sensed that someone had decided to make a preemptive strike before your budding alliance could form. In order to keep everyone alive, you cleared the stage. Isn't that it?"

He was mostly correct. If she were to append anything, it would be that she hadn't merely had some vague sense that someone was going to make a move—what she clearly sensed was the intent to kill. Monkey wasn't the only one who intended to put a swift end to the Zodiac War before the fighters ever left that starting room—but this person had decided on a completely opposite approach. Had Monkey delayed her response by a fraction of an instant, the battle might really have ended then and there.

"I see," Rat said. "And you don't know who wanted to kill everyone?"

"I don't," Monkey replied. "I didn't have time to find out. It was all I could do to escape—to let everyone escape."

"I said you can drop the modesty. I bet if you wanted to, you could have figured out who it was and taken them out instead of running away. Tell me I'm wrong."

"I won't say I couldn't have," Monkey admitted. "But I don't use my power like that. Great power must be used correctly."

"Correctly, eh? I think maybe whoever wanted to kill us had it correct. Their way would have ended the Zodiac War a whole lot quicker than this exhausting peace plan of yours. You go through all this time and trouble to make your peace negotiations and to offer your ceasefires, but don't you think that if you just wielded whatever power it is that you have to end this battle in an instant, you'd save more lives, and faster?"

Monkey was lost again. She asked, "What do you mean?"

"I mean—aside from yourself, think about what kind of people take part in the Zodiac War. What reason do you have to go and break your back over saving the lives of their kind? The world would be better off with all of us dead. That includes me. And if you're going to say that every life is equally precious, or that nobody is truly bad to the core, or some cliché like that, well, those are just hollow words from someone who won't face reality."

"If that's truly what you've decided," Monkey said, "then you'd better quit being a fighter right now. You don't have what it takes to fight."

The words came out a little more harshly than she'd intended. *Maybe he did provoke me after all.* Despite that vague realization, she continued, "You said no one in the world has saved as many people as I have. But no one else has *failed* to save as many as I have. There are many who I tried to save but couldn't. More than I could ever count. And more than I could ever forget."

Rat listened.

"I've seen countries destroyed," Monkey said. "I've seen senseless massacres. I've seen perversions of justice that are seared into the backs of my eyelids. I've seen humans hunted. I've seen slavery. I've seen treachery and betrayal. I've seen inhumane weapons, human trafficking, elders left to die in the wilderness. I've seen children kill their parents, and I've seen children culled. I've seen cultural suppression, the mass destruction of historical sites, natural resources exhausted, discrimination and prejudice. I've seen revenge strikes and counterattacks, male chauvinism and the subjection of women, famine and plague. I've seen all of it. I've seen it with no end. I've stared at it. I've seen reality. And after all that, here I am—still saying my 'hollow words.' Still having chosen my way. I chose to use the power of words not to end *a* war but to end *all* war. I've been through hell, but I still want us all to get along. I still want us all to be happy."

Then, gently, she added, "Don't underestimate my 'hollow words,' boy."

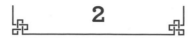

2

The boy had fallen back into silence—or rather, back into sleep. Monkey didn't think he was sulking, but she wondered if she had gone too far, and regretted it. Monkey thought, *Children really are hard to deal with.* And now that they were again only two, the uncomfortable silence hung in the air unbroken. No matter the grandiose words she spoke, no matter who called her a hero, how pathetic was she if she couldn't manage to communicate with one child? *That just goes to show how much I have yet to learn.* To the best of her inexperience, she thought about what to do next.

Monkey had been planning on waiting for everyone to calm back down before proposing her peace plan again, but if what Chicken had said about the state of things aboveground was to be believed—and Monkey had no choice but to believe it for now—then the Zodiac War was progressing at a far more rapid pace than the pacifist had expected. This battle had already seen three victims. If Rat's hunch was to be believed—and with nothing to substantiate it, Monkey still held reasonable doubts—then Chicken too was dead. Of the original twelve fighters, only Rat and Monkey and at most six others remained.

Maybe I was being too naïve, but I'm surprised that so many fighters are so actively engaged in killing. Even if the judge says we can have any wish fulfilled, isn't staying alive worth something? Besides, everyone here is resourceful enough to be able to fulfill most any wish through their own efforts.

Take Rabbit, for example. From what Chicken had told Monkey before leaving for the surface, the man was a necromanticist who could command the dead in battle. With that kind of power, there was little he could want that he couldn't get for himself. What reason then did he have to risk his life to fight? Sure, once nominated for the Zodiac War, participation was compulsory—that was an invitation one dared not decline—but she had expected to see a difference in the actions of the fighters who approached the game with eagerness and those who did so with reluctance. That was why the people in charge took steps to keep the Zodiac War moving, such as making the combatants swallow poison jewels. But judging by the pace the warriors were setting, such steps seemed hardly necessary.

Do I wait a little longer and watch for the right opportunity? Or do I go aboveground now? I need to make a decision.

And then she didn't need to make a decision. Rather, she didn't have the chance to make one.

There came a loud noise, amplified by the echoes of the narrow sewer passages, and too loud to be ignored. The echoes masked the direction of the sound's source, but wherever it was, it was coming closer.

"Nezumi, wake up!"

Rat groaned and said, "Just five more minutes."

Monkey kicked him.

"Ow! I thought you were against violence." Rat sat up. "Wait, what's that noise? Sounds like a helicopter or something."

A helicopter could never have been in the sewers, but that was what it most sounded like—like something was cutting through the air, repeatedly, relentlessly, and chopping through it again. The noises overlapped and affected each other. Did that mean this was more than one thing coming toward them?

Monkey's deductions ended there. Before she could find the answer, far faster than her mind could work, the answer found her—though even if she had more time to think, she might never have imagined what it was. In everything she had seen in all the world's battlefields, she had never seen anything like this.

The sound belonged to wings—the flapping wings of a great flock of birds. Rather, the flapping wings of a great flock of *dead* birds.

The zombie mass swarmed through the tunnel and found Monkey and Rat. Then, as if holding the pair in their sights, the birds hovered in place.

Monkey froze in shock, but impressively, her mind worked to make the connection. "Is this…the necromanticist's work? He's using the dead birds?"

Monkey's deductions were limited by the vague snippets she'd heard of what had happened on the surface. What she didn't know was that these were Chicken's birds—the birds felled by the nonstop barrage of Boar's twin machine guns when Chicken summoned the Sky Burial. The key point there was that Boar's bullets had killed the winged animals, and at the time, Boar was under Rabbit's control. This signified two crucial facts: the necromanticist's ability to command those he killed was not restricted to human targets, and this ability extended not only to those killed by his hand, but those killed by his minions as well—though of course, he would call those reanimated corpses his *friends*.

While whatever they were called was a matter of personal preference, one fact remained: the few dozen birds Boar had killed before being consumed by the flock were now obeying that vile necromanticist, not Chicken.

The birds hovered with wounded wings that splattered blood all around with each flap. The undead creatures caught Monkey speechless—not by the sight of their busted beaks or their claws fractured into something even sharper than they once were, but because of the person controlling them with no respect for the dead animals and no regard for the sanctity of life.

I understand the logic—while normal birds would never enter the sewers, their corpses would have no such qualms against the search. But there's more to the world than logic.

The tactic gave no sign of fastidiousness, just an inhumanly cold and systematic logic: if I do A, then B will happen, therefore I will do A.

"This is bad," Rat said. His voice remained sleepy as always, but his expression was serious. That must have just been how he naturally spoke. "There's too many of them. Even if we don't get killed, if we try to fight this many small animals in such an enclosed space, we're sure to get hurt. And in a filthy place like this, we'll have a very high chance of getting a tetanus infection."

Monkey knew as much—that risk was one reason she had agreed to hide out down in the sewers. In a way, being unsuited for fighting made the place something of a neutral territory. But when their opponents were already dead, that mental impediment only applied to one side.

"We're running," Monkey said as she seized the child by the nape of his neck and broke into a sprint. The dead flock didn't pursue them immediately. Monkey figured that was just because the corpses needed a little more time to get moving, but that didn't change the danger the two were in should they remain underground.

"Let go of me. I can run on my own," Rat said, embarrassed, but Monkey ignored his protests and bolted up the nearest ladder, lifted the manhole cover, and emerged—into the oncoming slash of a blade.

But Monkey had expected the attack and was ready with the right response. Narrowly dodging the blow, she unleashed a swift kick at the back of her opponent's neck—but her attack was also narrowly dodged. Except it shouldn't have been. Her shin should have slammed into her enemy's neck. Despite being known as a pacifist, Monkey excelled at hand-to-hand combat. She could hit any target with her eyes closed.

But her attack couldn't hit a neck when there was no neck where one was supposed to be. Instead, her kick passed through air.

Another corpse, Monkey thought, as she and Rat rolled across the pavement. *This one is Snake. But that blade doesn't belong to him.*

"Ow," Rat groaned, but Monkey was getting back on her feet. She faced her opponents.

Standing beside Snake was the man with the freakish expression and the freakish attire—Rabbit. Of the two, the corpse—the headless corpse, at that—was the less disturbing. With an unsteady arm, the puppet returned the giant blade to its owner, who now held one in each hand.

Rabbit announced himself.

"I am Usagi, the Fighter of the Rabbit. I kill with distinction."

Monkey could clearly see this was no time to bid for a truce, at least not how things stood now.

She thought, *This leaves me no choice*, then said, "Nezumi, can I leave Snake to you?"

"What, you're fighting now?"

"I'm a pacifist, but I'm no adherent to nonresistance. I'm going to restrain him without injuring him, and I'll get him to understand."

"Restrain him without injuring him? You know that's a lot harder than just taking him down." Rat sighed. "You do this every time."

"What do you mean I do this every time?"

"I mean always. No matter what happens." The boy got to his feet. "All right. I'll handle him."

Monkey wasn't sure how good a fighter Rat was, but no matter his age, a warrior was a warrior. He almost certainly wouldn't be killed instantly by a corpse. Even if he didn't win, he would at least be able to draw the fight out long enough for her to incapacitate Rabbit.

Not that I know how I'm going to incapacitate a necromanticist...

Simply disarming him of those two massive blades wouldn't likely be enough. In the meantime, she and Rat took their fighting stances and readied themselves for the battle.

"I am Sharyū, the Fighter of the Monkey. I kill in peace."

"I am Nezumi, the Fighter of the Rat. I kill inexorably."

The first to move was, surprisingly, the slowest moving of

the four—Snake's corpse. And he was moving to leave. Apparently, both sides were looking for a one-on-one battle. Rat took his cue and followed the walking corpse.

Keeping one eye on the pair's departure, Monkey said to Rabbit, even though she knew it was futile, "You raised your hand back in that high-rise, didn't you? It's not too late to work together with us. You remember what I said, right? I can save all of us. If you can find it in yourself to have a change of heart, and you'll listen to me, then…"

Was he listening? Monkey couldn't tell. Whatever emotion lurked behind Rabbit's expression, she couldn't read it.

Monkey pressed on. "If you're trying to win because you want your wish granted, we'd be more than happy to help you make it come true. If we all work together, no dream will be beyond our reach."

Still nothing. Monkey was perplexed by the lack of any response whatsoever from the man, but quickly she learned that he simply hadn't been listening at all.

She shouldn't have left that manhole cover open.

A swarm of birds flew out from the hole.

He wasn't listening to me—he was waiting for his underground reinforcements to arrive. And he didn't want a one-on-one fight, he just wanted to split us up.

His strategy was without regard for anything else and devoid of even an iota of emotional attachment, as if he were putting together a jigsaw puzzle. To call it machinelike wouldn't quite have been right. He was working chess pieces on a board—or rather, Othello pieces, where each is indistinguishable and only position matters. There was no humanity in it at all.

Monkey had negotiated with all manner of people, but this man's values were so alien to her that he might as well have been from outer space.

Undaunted, unwavering, Monkey persisted, "Rabbit, is your wish—"

But then the roar of flapping wings drowned out her voice.

The birds rushed her, and no words could dissuade their attack. At least here, aboveground, she wouldn't have to worry about getting some terrible infection, but the animals' beaks and talons were still dangerous enough on their own.

This leaves me no choice!

Monkey steadied her resolve and began slapping down the dead birds as they assailed her from all directions. From a distance, she appeared only to be flailing wildly, but in reality, her movements were calculated, and she struck the mock-phoenixes one by one, sending them slamming to the ground. Not every attack connected with her winged enemies, but even those would-be misses were feint attacks designed to restrict and guide the birds' movements. The strikes that landed didn't simply drop the creatures either, but broke their wings so that they wouldn't take flight again.

Monkey considered her opponent's fighting style inhuman, but her own technique was superhuman. Even in the sewer, she might have been able to fight with equal success— except there, she had been accompanied by a child and decided to act with caution.

With moves so smooth they seemed choreographed, she wielded her hands like knives and chopped down the birds one after another. But inside, her emotions were not so poised.

Dead or not, attacking these little creatures feels wrong.

Was that Rabbit's plan all along? Had he sent the birds in first to mentally weaken her?

Just as the birds were nearly all felled, and Monkey began to feel a moment of relief, the main challenger struck. He came in low, swinging his massive blades in an attempt cut her torso in half.

He's going for my stomach, Monkey realized—an unfeeling attack, as if her body was nothing but a container for her jewel inside. *That mindset is as grave a danger as I've ever seen—but his skill is not on that same level.*

His fighting skills weren't just on a lesser level—they weren't even close. His swing was that of an amateur, if anything. It seemed his decision to have Snake ambush her as she came up from the manhole hadn't just been to safeguard himself from a possible counterattack, but to cover for his own deficiencies.

Well, a necromanticist has little need to be a master swordsman—but his not being one will save my life.

The birds had indeed thrown her mental state into some small amount of disorder, and were she facing someone of, say, Ox's caliber, she might have been in danger.

Monkey leaped high into the air, passing above the horizontal swing of the twin blades, and then even above Rabbit's head, finally landing behind his back. She could see—from not just how he handled his weapons, but also from the placement of his feet and the way he moved his body—that he was no master fighter. Unlike Monkey, he lacked the expertise to respond to an attack from behind—and she wouldn't give him the time to turn around. She moved to pin him down—her thoughts were already on how she would incapacitate him, how to subdue him, and how to convince him to see her way, when she heard him say,

"Got you."

And she felt two objects inside her, and her thoughts stopped in their tracks.

"What?" she said.

She didn't need to see his twin blades to know they were what impaled her, but she couldn't help herself from looking. When she did, she wished she hadn't.

There they were, deep inside her fragile body—too deep. They looked more like two handles sprouting from her flesh.

Without turning, Rabbit had twisted his wrists to drive those two massive blades into her, each passing cleanly into each of her lungs. Derailed though her thoughts had been, it was clear to see that these wounds were fatal. Whether she would die first from asphyxiation or loss of blood was anyone's guess, but she was going to die.

How—how did he do that? Where did that come from?

He had failed to cut open her stomach to reach the poison jewel within, but still, it was a masterful strike. Had he been putting on an act to trick her into believing he was an amateur? Was it a feint? Monkey didn't think so. If he was that good at putting on a performance, he should have been an actor, not a fighter. What was it then?

As the strength seeped from her body, she slumped forward onto the blades that were still lodged in her lungs. She went limp, and her shoulders fell back, along with her head, and then she found the answer.

A short distance away from where they fought, dangling like a giant fruit from the limb of a roadside tree, was a severed head—recognizable to anyone who had been there at the start of the game. It was Snake's head.

That's right…the Snake that went off with Rat was just a headless body. Meanwhile, she had known nothing of the whereabouts of the bodyless head. But what should it have mattered? A body without a head could still do something, at least, but what could a head without a body accomplish?

But Rabbit had found a use for it. He suspended it from a tree branch to make an impromptu surveillance camera—one that could watch his back. One that could protect him.

Without turning, Rabbit said, "It's nice to have a friend that you can trust will have your six. It's really, really nice."

Then he continued, "It's going to be all right. Don't be afraid. I'm only going to take your life. But in exchange, I want you to be my friend too. You know, I always liked you, from the moment I first saw you."

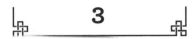

3

At the start of the Zodiac War, when Monkey was looking for friends to join with her, and Rabbit raised his hand, not one person in the room believed his offer was genuine. Not even Monkey, the pacifist at heart, completely believed his intentions were true. But when it came to wanting to befriend her, he had been uncharacteristically sincere. And now, Team Rabbit had its newest member—the shadow of a hero, bereft of the pacifism more precious to her than her own life.

RABBIT VS. ~~MONKEY~~
END OF THE 4ᵀᴴ BATTLE

THE FIFTH BATTLE

"A wolf in sheep's clothing."

**HITSUJII,
THE FIGHTER
OF THE SHEEP**

"I wish for time."

REAL NAME: Sumihiko TSUJIIE
BORN: August 8
HEIGHT: 140 cm
WEIGHT: 40 kg

Sumihiko used to be an arms dealer who only frequented war zones to make his sales, but after repeatedly getting caught in the flames of war, he began to distinguish himself as a fighter. Eventually, he caught the eye of a daughter in the family of one of his clients, the Tsujiie clan, and he was married into the clan.

The days when he traveled far and wide selling arms are long past, as is the fighting; for some time now Sumihiko has remained away from the front lines. But when he learned that his beloved grandchild was going to be chosen for the Zodiac War, he volunteered himself first.

This is his second Zodiac War—his previous being the ninth—and he was, obviously, the winner. (His wish: to see his grandchild.) In his active years, he wielded all manner of heavy weaponry to terrific and destructive effect, but lately he's taken to grenades. He oversees the manufacture of his own custom grenade, *Shūkaiokuri*, the Old-Timer, which he boasts of as more of a work of art than a weapon.

Though the habit is unseemly for one his age, he is addicted to smartphone games and often tops the biggest spender lists of the most popular games. Through his online persona, the old man has once again found fame as a highly respected warrior.

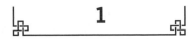

1

Hitsujii, the Fighter of the Sheep, thought, *If the twelve fighters participating in this battle were ranked by overall strength, even the most charitable assessment would place me at tenth or worse. After all, youth is strength. Damn, how I wish I could stop getting older.*

But age alone wasn't the whole of his problems. As times changed and new generations came to prominence, fighting styles and tactics changed in equal measure. In the high-rise, he had observed the other eleven fighters one by one and was struck by how many seemed alien to him and unlike any warriors of his day—of course to one another, they were nothing unusual. He was a relic from another time; not just aged but *old*. In the intervening years, fighters had evolved and left him behind. That was the way of the world.

But he didn't believe this put him at a significant disadvantage—just as the others were inscrutable to him, he was as inscrutable to them. Likewise, if the others possessed advantages he lacked, so too did he possess advantages they lacked.

Of those, I have more than I could count, but the foremost is experience.

Monkey might have saved more lives than any other combatant there, but none had seen as many battles as Sheep. He had escaped death so many times that he'd have liked to tell the organizers a thing or two about the tame rules they cooked up for this Zodiac War. That sentiment only reinforced the feeling that the times had changed.

I won't make that tired complaint, "The old days were better," and all that—the present is better as a matter of course. For one thing, soldiers have fought hard to make the world a safer place.

As long as humans walked the earth, war would never cease. A mercenary would never be without employ. But the kinds of battlefields Sheep saw on the front lines of war— or before that, when he worked as an arms dealer—with mountains of corpses and rivers of blood, were nowhere to be found anymore.

This was a good thing, but thinking about it made him feel lonely. Over the course of his long life, he had come to see the passing of time from a more distant perspective, as if gazing upon a landscape. This too was an advantage exclusive to Sheep.

Another was information, which in the Zodiac War was practically life. Sheep knew who his eleven rivals were. He knew exactly to which houses they belonged—actually, that wasn't quite true. He knew of ten, but the last was a simple process of elimination. The only combatant about whom he hadn't managed to dig up any information was the Fighter of the Rat, who must have been the kid.

Well, some wet-behind-the-ears whippersnapper won't have any history on or off the battlefield for me to find.

Now that he'd observed his opponents in person, he didn't merely rely upon his research, but fine-tuned his mental dossiers.

Of the competitors this time around, three stand out as unquestionably the top fighters in the world: the Fighter of the Monkey, Sharyū; the Fighter of the Rabbit, Usagi; and the Fighter of the

Ox, Ushii. When you assemble twelve people together, some are bound to possess talents far surpassing the rest—but these three are just beyond.

Sheep didn't know if the trio had been brought here by chance or by purposeful design—but whatever the case, Sheep knew he mustn't face them head on.

I'm just skin and bones—I wouldn't last ten seconds against them. But if I can arrange it so they destroy one another, even a feeble old fighter like me would have a real shot at winning.

According to Sheep's analysis, after taking his opponents' personalities into account, Ox stood unsurprisingly at the top. Nearly as dangerous at number two was Rabbit, and the pacifist Monkey ranked third. If he hadn't factored in her character, Monkey would likely have claimed the top spot, but Sheep couldn't imagine that a hero like Monkey would ever betray her pacifist ways.

Boar, of the previous winning house, is fourth, and Horse and Dog, who both seem the up-close-and-personal types, share fifth and sixth. In seventh and eighth are the twins, Dragon and Snake—or at least they were, when they came as a set. With Snake as the first dead, Dragon's placement will surely drop. For now, I'll slot Chicken in ninth.

At the starting point, only Chicken had observed the other fighters with the same eye as Sheep. She recognized that she lacked strength and was seeking to turn her weakness into an advantage. The woman was making the necessary effort to turn her weakness from the reason she wouldn't win into the reason she could win.

She would likely rank herself at the very bottom, though I would never agree. For now, I'll give myself tenth place, leaving the only two I can say for a fact are weaker than me: Rat and Tiger. Tiger is so lacking I can't even fathom what she's doing here.

Rat was young—too young—and even if he could have somehow squeezed Sheep's life experience into his own, the child would have been prone to making careless misjudgments, and as such, the old man didn't see much hope for him. But Tiger didn't even seem like she belonged here. Of course, there must have been something about her that earned her a place in the Zodiac War. That might have been enough cause for Sheep to reassess her threat, but he dismissed it. He needed to look toward those above him, not those below. How could he surpass the nine who ranked higher than him? How could he close the gap that separated him from them? Those were the questions he asked himself.

With my experience and the knowledge upon which it's founded, that's how. And…if I have another advantage, it's this.

In the palm of his hand, he idly rolled the murky-black jewel—the so-called beast gem, the poisonous crystal he had never swallowed.

2

To be young was not to know fear—and to be obe-
dient. When told to take the jewels, they took; when
told to swallow the jewels, they swallowed. If courage and
open-mindedness were to blame, then Sheep had discarded
those concerns a long time ago. He knew that to live was to
be cautious, and to survive was to avoid taking risks—and to
live was to win.

Sheep wasn't a master poisoner and hadn't recognized the
jewels for what they were, but precisely because he couldn't
identify the objects, he let the other fighters take theirs first,
and no matter the orders of that silk-hatted judge, Sheep
didn't swallow his jewel. The moment the Duodecuple said,
"However, I'm going to have to ask you to swallow only one,"
Sheep concluded that those little orbs were dangerous.

And so he only pretended to swallow his, instead stowing
it in his breast pocket. Compared to some of his competitors'
actions, like Chicken's Eye of the Cormorant and Sky Burial,
which technically speaking called in the help of outside ac-
tors and might have been considered by some as a breach of
the rules—or at least as occupying a gray area—Sheep's dis-
obedience was a clear and flagrant violation. Even Dog, who
neutralized his poison within his body, was a different story.
If anyone had noticed Sheep's actions, he would have been
immediately disqualified. In other words, Sheep, informed by
his life experiences, determined that the risk of obeying the

instructions and swallowing the jewel outweighed the risk of getting caught.

If I had to identify the tipping point, Sheep thought, *it was that the jewel's cut seemed unnatural. The murky-black color had a beauty to it, but the cut did not.*

Call it a sense for aesthetics cultivated over his long life. He had been right; the jewel's cut wasn't for appearance's sake but to prevent the fighters from regurgitating the crystals. By not panicking when told they had just swallowed poison, his opponents showed themselves to be warriors—but as far as Sheep was concerned, a true warrior would never swallow poison.

This means that I alone am free from the time limit. But I can't let this advantage tempt me into remaining frivolously idle.

Dog, having neutralized his poison, had decided to keep himself hidden until his foes were nearly out of time. Sheep was not clairvoyant, nor did he have the Eye of the Cormorant, and had no way of knowing Chicken had upturned Dog's strategy. Nevertheless, Sheep chose to pursue a different approach. Unlike Dog, who possessed absolute faith in his strength in combat and the power of his fangs, the old man ranked himself in tenth place or below. A poor fighter in perfect health was not guaranteed a victory over a top fighter weakened by poison—or at least that was how Sheep saw it.

Also, unlike Dog, Sheep had committed a serious violation of the rules. If he waited out a prolonged battle, he risked exposing his transgression, which would mean immediate disqualification. Even if his strategic goal remained the same as Dog's—to let the stronger fighters kill each other off—he couldn't merely sit around and wait for it to happen.

That's why I need to put this advantage to work in another fashion. I have in my hand a jewel that everyone else has swallowed. I can use it as a bargaining chip.

He needed to go after someone in the middling ranks—ideally somewhere around fourth, fifth, or sixth place—someone not particularly worried about losing, but who must have also devised a strategy to compete with the top three who stood so far above the rest. A fighter in that position would be seeking an ace in the hole. By offering that ace, Sheep might be able to secure himself that thing that every fighter wanted but only rarely seemed to find—an alliance.

Of course it's clear to see that as long as there can be only one winner, any alliance, and any form of cooperation, will collapse at the end. But I know of a way to preserve that relationship until the last possible moment.

Sheep might have been the only fighter who could use that method. When he decided not to swallow his jewel, he paid close attention to the other fighters to see who swallowed theirs—and all, save for the already dead Snake, had indeed ingested the poison.

And no matter how calm and collected these people may try to act, I know they're anxious— even if they might be a natural, like Ox, or a hero. Not only do they have to battle one another, they are fighting against the pressure of knowing they must win before the poison kills them. Maybe, due to some blunder on the part of the organizers, their poison will act more quickly than intended. Or maybe, rather than just react to the poison, their bodies will have an allergic reaction to the foreign objects. No matter how resolute the fighters may be, once that poison is waiting in their stomachs, there's no end to the doubts and worries.

The poisoned fighters wouldn't be able to remain sound in mind or body—well, except for the ones who weren't sound in the first place, like Rabbit, but aside from such exceptional exceptions, some crack would appear. And into that crack Sheep would strike—but with a gentle touch.

Sheep ran through the scenario in his mind.

First he would establish contact with a fighter in fourth place or below on his list, and then he would attempt to make a deal—while displaying the poison gem in his hand. He already knew what he would say.

"With my special power, I can manipulate quantum tunnels at will and enable objects of my choosing to pass through solid matter."

This, of course, was a complete lie. Whatever special combat powers he might have once possessed had faded to nothing over the years—no necromanticism or Eye of the Cormorant for him—but pretending he had something he lacked was easier than pretending to lack something he had. After all, he held an object that was supposed to be in his stomach—convincing his mark that he had reached past his skin, flesh, and organs to pull out the jewel was entirely possible, if he sold it right.

Because Sheep had encountered a soldier with a similar ability in the past, he could bring a certain air of truth to the lie. This was where he needed to put his life experience to work—otherwise, if his target began to have an inkling of doubt, his tale would fall apart.

But this was merely his lead-in. To simply announce that he was free of the poison would earn him only animosity, but if he were to offer, "I can remove yours from your body without causing you any harm," then a negotiation could start.

Of course, he wouldn't be removing the jewel from anyone's stomach—for one thing, such a feat was impossible for him, and for another, he didn't want to. But regardless of his actual intent, the offer would be too tempting for anyone to resist.

The key factor here was that the mark wouldn't likely say, "All right, go ahead and take my jewel out." After all, a stolen crystal meant a stolen victory. As long as the time limit wasn't a concern, where better to safeguard their jewel than inside one's own body? Because of this, Sheep's offer would be seen as insurance to be used only when necessary.

His target might try to test him in other ways, like by asking him to use his ability to steal the jewels of other fighters, but Sheep would just have to do his best to handle that as it came—and, as the dominant partner in any arrangement, he'd have some room to maneuver.

Sheep also wouldn't be seeking to expand his team beyond one partner. He needed to inveigle one person to his side; no more and no less. Even two would be inviting danger. Had his made-up superpower been real, the size of his alliance wouldn't have mattered, but it wasn't real. If he tried to lie to two people, and they talked, the incongruities in his story would be irrevocably revealed. It was a strange but true fact: those incapable of seeing when they were being deceived were still perceptive of deception against others.

This lie was, after all, an attempt to skate on thin ice—one that could be exposed by a single cautious demand: "Prove it by using your power on something else." He needed to minimize every possible risk.

But Sheep figured a team of two would be enough. With Snake and Dragon split up at the very beginning, the only fighter left capable of assembling an alliance was Monkey—and even if she managed to put a team together, an alliance of pacifists gave him no cause for concern. Numbers alone were just that—numbers.

If I could have my way, I'd aim for someone in the middle ranks, like fourth through sixth—but under the right circumstances, I might need to approach someone weaker.

It's been three hours since the Zodiac War began. The time should be right for me to stir things up.

Having waited for the right timing, Sheep decided to set out in search of his mark. At almost the same time, in another place in the ghost city, the top-ranking fighters were indeed clashing. In that sense, his timing was as right as he figured it to be. But the results of that clash—a zombified Monkey teaming up with the decidedly non-pacifist Rabbit—was not in accordance with his wishes. No amount of life experience would ever have led Sheep to predict the emergence of such an alliance.

3

Before Sheep was a soldier, he had been an arms dealer and excelled at clandestine operations. He might have been even better at hiding than he was at fighting. Dog had failed to remain hidden, even though he stayed in his hiding place, but not even Chicken's Eye of the Cormorant would have easily tracked Sheep's movements as the diminutive old man dashed from shadow to shadow. He was careful not to allow himself to be seen from any angle, including from above—not because he knew of Chicken's power (his investigations never revealed that) but because that was how he always acted as a matter of course. At this moment, Chicken was being given her own Sky Burial, but that was beside the point.

In any event, only ten minutes after beginning his search, Sheep stopped and ducked into the shadow of a tree. The old soldier was an excellent tracker, but such swift results came as a surprise even to him. He didn't think it would be this easy to find another fighter. He'd assumed that after the floor fell out in the high-rise and the eleven combatants scattered, each would go into hiding and would wait for the chance to strike, as a tiger waited out its prey. He had expected to find the contest in an eleven-way deadlock, with each fighter hiding to the best of their abilities, and had steeled himself for a long and painstaking search—but no such grand effort was required to find this one.

She was not one of the necromanticist's walking corpses—the difference between someone living and someone dead was apparent enough even without a seasoned soldier's eye. Though Sheep didn't know about Rabbit's special ability, if the old man had come across one of the zombies, he would have at least sensed that something was odd—and he got no such sense from the woman drowning herself in booze on the park bench. There was an oddity to the situation, of course—a fighter going on a drinking binge in the middle of a battle was certainly no normal sight, and even less so when that fighter was a young woman.

It was the Fighter of the Tiger.

The one I listed at the very bottom. Teaming up with her might not be what I'm looking for, to say the least.

He thought about leaving and pretending he'd never seen her. Not only was running across her a minor disaster by itself, but he also felt like he was watching something illicit. Surrounding her bench was a massive pile of sake bottles—likely plundered from some abandoned liquor store—and a majority of the bottles were already empty. The drunk, scantily clad woman sat splayed across the bench with her legs spread wide. Red-faced and humming, enjoying herself, she tossed aside an empty bottle, then picked up a new one, removed the cap, and guzzled its contents straight from the source. These were the actions of a bum, not a warrior.

This is no tiger waiting for its prey—she's just going on a bender.

The vast divide between her namesake and actions provided a surrealistic effect. Although, back in the day, raging drunkards used to be called "big tigers" in some parts—not that a woman young as Tiger would have known such dated lingo.

I'd already ranked her at the bottom—I never expected to have to revise my opinion even lower. She doesn't feel anything like a threat—in fact, the only thing I feel for her is contempt.

Even had it made sense to ally with her, he wouldn't have wanted to. Sheep might have generally avoided saying, "Things used to be better," but he'd vowed never to start a complaint with "Kids these days…" Seeing Tiger, he almost broke that vow—even though, from a certain viewpoint, her behavior was a product of the peaceful times he otherwise appreciated.

If they weren't in the midst of a battle royale, he'd have liked to walk up to her and give her a good scolding—not as a warrior, but as a human being—but of course that wasn't an option now. This was no time for some old man's sermon. He needed to discard his emotions and remain focused on the battle.

But if I leave here and search out another warrior, I certainly won't just stumble across one so easily as I did this time—and the next might not be easy to bargain with.

The alternative was to prioritize urgency and to regard her with a more positive attitude—weak also meant easily coerced. Having her as his puppet might make for a valid strategy. Plus, he was not looking to form an alliance, but rather to devise a partnership under pretense, and a stupider target would be an easier mark—and would pose less risk of asking any tough questions. But even with that in mind, there were limits.

I'm not sure I could convince someone that drunk of anything—and she's so far gone, I'm not sure we could even converse.

That being the case, he considered whether attacking her might be a better option. Ambushing someone that vulnerable would wound his conscience—or at least, his warrior's pride—but battle itself was a disgrace all warriors had to bear.

She had made herself so defenseless, she was almost begging him to kill her. If Sheep spared her, another fighter would just come along and kill her instead. However little he cared about her fate, the jewel inside her body had real value. If he killed her and retrieved that sake-soaked jewel, he could use it for extra leverage when it came time to make a deal with someone else.

Since all twelve gems were needed to win the Zodiac War, logically it didn't matter who possessed any jewel in the meantime—but if someone told him to take one, he'd have heard worse suggestions. He could also use it to imply his strength and standing in the game—as long as he could hide the fact he stole it from someone so soused.

So that's it then. I'm not the warrior I used to be, and I'd hoped to avoid any fighting until the very end, but...

His thoughts ever humble, Sheep resolved himself to action. He reached for a grenade—the Shūkaiokuri he'd developed to give him the edge he needed to win—when the drunken tiger said gruffly, "I know you're there. Quit your peeping and get your ass out in the open, old man."

4

Dwarfing Sheep's initial surprise at being detected was the bigger shock that Tiger could still form complete sentences even after emptying that many sake bottles. He had assumed she was either at or near blackout-level drunkenness.

The woman said, her voice a low growl, "Aren't you a little old to play hide-and-seek? If you want to play, I'll play with you, tiger. Tiger, get it?"

Maybe she could talk, but it was still the words of a lush. Sheep had raised his guard for a moment, but that seemed unnecessary now. Drunks could notice the most peculiar things; maybe he had just happened to stray into her field of view.

"Well then, miss," Sheep said, "I'll play your game. It would be rude of me to turn down a young lady's invitation."

Making himself appear larger than he was—even a small man could seem bigger with the right stride—Sheep stepped from the shadow of the tree where he had been hiding. In response, Tiger stood from her bench—or at least, she tried to stand and then toppled over. Sheep wondered, albeit warily, if he had won without a fight.

Instead, she got on all fours. That she didn't stay down was all right with him. Had the fight been settled there, before they could even announce their names, it would have been too much of a letdown.

If this form—on her hands and knees—was how she typically fought, Sheep was impressed that she had survived as long as she had in life. From that stance, her first move was restricted to scratching with her claws. A skilled hawk hid its talons, but apparently this Tiger hadn't the same sense. With this approach, she might have been stone sober and the result would be nearly the same.

She growled—not very ladylike at all—and said, "Whoa, your mirror image technique is incredible, old man. You can make there be three of you."

Sheep didn't know what she was seeing, but he knew what he saw—a red-faced, miserable excuse for a warrior. It was time to put an end to this. For a moment there, he had thought he might get some thrill out of his first real fight in a long time, but it looked like he was wrong.

"Huh?" Tiger slurred. "Wait, when did there get to be four of you?" Another growl. "Oh, I get it, one sheep, two sheep, huh? You're trying to put me to sleep, is that it?"

"Perhaps we should introduce ourselves once you're a little less drunk, miss."

He'd offered her a way out on reflex, so lackluster an opponent was she. If she really did fall asleep on the spot, he wouldn't have been surprised.

"Shut up, I'm not drunk," she said, exactly as a drunk would. "I'm not drunk, I'm not. Just a little bit drunk. I can drink all the sake I want and be just fine."

Whatever pity he still had for her wouldn't have filled a single sake cup. With his Old-Timer Shūkaiokuri grenades, he'd obliterate any traces of her except the contents of her stomach. The grenades' destructive power was absolute—back in the high-rise, when he had decided to utilize the explosives to end the Zodiac War as soon as it started, even Monkey had to crumble the floor to escape.

But Monkey was one thing—this half-asleep woman was another. He wouldn't misfire this time.

"I am Hitsujii, the Fighter of the Sheep. I kill with deception."

"I am Tora, the Fighter of the Tiger. I kill with drunken power."

Drunken power? he began to question, but it was already too late. Her clawing attack—the obvious move—should have been easy to dodge. But the next thing he knew, all ten of her nails raked his little body, ripping off his skin, shredding every part of him except his stomach.

What? Sheep thought, too lost in confusion to realize these were his dying moments. *What? She was supposed to be at the bottom. Even when she announced her name, nothing changed in her—no surge of power or anything. From the top of her head to the tips of her toes, she was just a drunk. Wait...a drunk? Could it be?*

From somewhere behind him, she said, "I see you've heard of the Drunken Fist. You know, that same old standby—the more I drink, the stronger I get. But you know what, old man—you fit the visual better than me. Funny thing." She punctuated it with another growl, then fell to the ground even before Sheep did.

This time, she didn't try to get back up. Instead, she licked her blood-soaked nails, and her face took on a look of insatiable ecstasy.

"In my case, human blood gets me much drunker than sake. But one little old man won't be enough to satisfy me."

Tiger went on the move.

TIGER VS. ~~SHEEP~~
END OF THE 5ᵀᴴ BATTLE

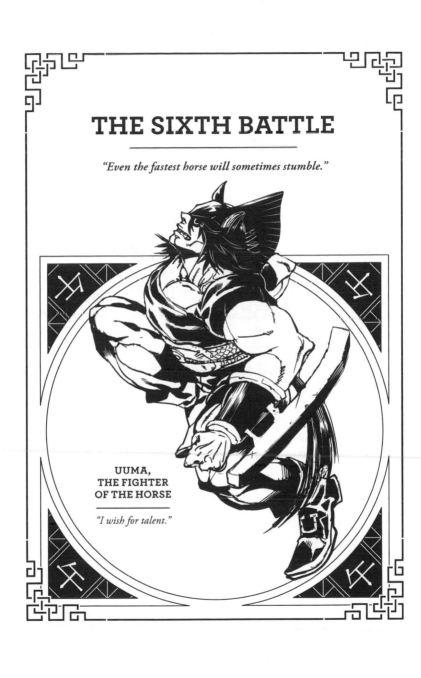

THE SIXTH BATTLE

"Even the fastest horse will sometimes stumble."

**UUMA,
THE FIGHTER
OF THE HORSE**

"I wish for talent."

REAL NAME: **Yoshimi SŌMA**
BORN: **September 9**
HEIGHT: **230 cm**
WEIGHT: **150 kg**

In his teens, Yoshimi was tall but slender, but after experiencing a decisive defeat in battle, he took up bodybuilding. He augmented his physical training by unhesitatingly reaching out for drugs to alter his body chemistry. The result is the most physically massive man in the history of the Sōma clan.

He is known as a man of few words, and only his closest associates have heard him speak, aside from when he announces his name before battle. (As a fact of little relevance to this document, he has a very nice voice.)

In battle, he fights with a stoicism befitting his quiet nature. It goes without saying that the attacks launched by those powerful muscles are extraordinary, but most notable is his defense. He has a special ability he calls "Stirrup," which can increase the toughness of his body beyond normal human limits.

Incidentally, he intended to name this ability the rather unremarkable "Armor," but he made a mistake when writing the kanji. Luckily, it still fits him rather well.

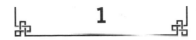

1

The Zodiac War, held once every twelve years—now that only half the participants remain, allow me to reveal what I can of the inner workings of the Zodiac Wars.

As I'm sure you've guessed, the chosen warriors do not stake their lives and souls in a bloody contest of ability, talent, skill, and sometimes luck simply to determine which among them is the strongest. For one thing, the Zodiac War militates against good sportsmanship, but its hidden workings are perhaps even uglier and more unsavory than its gory surface.

There is a reason these fighters, who normally do battle in war zones across the world, are assembled to compete in the same place.

When the organizers of this Zodiac War sacrificed an entire city to serve as the battle's stage, the measure wasn't some atypical extravagance or splurge. For one past Zodiac War, they destroyed an entire mountain range; for the ninth—the largest-scale event so far—they utilized a space station. Not only do the organizers go to great expense to prepare the battlegrounds, the prize—the granting of any single wish—could, depending on the wish, be of astronomical cost.

The organizers go to such extreme lengths to hold these Zodiac Wars, at the not so infrequent timing of once every twelve years, because it serves as a war via proxy.

The Zodiac War is held at a great cost of wealth, lives, and land, but only fought by twelve chosen warriors. The imbalance is, on its face, absurd. But the twelve fighters don't fight as representatives of any particular nation; in fact, nations are nothing more than gambling chips in the hands of the ultra-elite.

A few individuals, wielding far more power than any country, compete for nations in a fair and controlled manner—for example, a Chicken win could be worth two countries; a Monkey win with Ox in second could be worth three. Depending on the results of the Zodiac War, nations can change owners, be created or destroyed, or merge or gain independence. The world map is redrawn.

Of course, the twelve fighters know nothing of this arrangement. Each puts their life on the line for their own reasons.

The betting takes place once six warriors remain, as they've now had sufficient time to display their strengths. For the Twelfth Zodiac War, the survivors' odds have been ranked as follows:

1) Ox
2) Rabbit
3) Tiger
4) Horse
5) Dragon
6) Rat

Having shown astounding ability in his fight against Chicken, Ox has secured his place in the lead as many had expected of him, but Rabbit's position in second comes as something of an upset. This is undoubtedly due to his powers as a necromanticist. Depending on how effectively he puts his two corpse followers to use, he has a solid chance at victory. Both he and Ox are far ahead of the pack.

As for the rest, Tiger, in third, also came into the contest with no expectations, but her defeat of the veteran among veterans was the likely cause for reconsideration. Dragon ranks low not because of anything he has done, but because he has lost his brother and partner. And Rat—on the one hand, he's seen as too young, and on the other, he's shown no interest in the fighting. Neither Dragon nor Rat has performed any noteworthy actions in the contest thus far, but Dragon likely places the higher of the two because at least something is known of his ability. The same can't be said for Rat.

But what I want to focus on is not them, but the fighter in fourth place, which is not a good ranking, but also certainly not bad—neither a sure bet nor a long shot, but a bet with average odds. I'm talking about Uuma, the Fighter of the Horse.

In a survey conducted before this Zodiac War, the elite betters ranked Horse near the very top of the competitors. In a battle royale, where survival means victory, his impenetrable defense—equated by some to the aegis shield of lore—should be a considerable advantage.

Why then, at the halfway point, has he failed to follow through on expectations? The answer comes next in the story—but before you read on, perhaps you would like to consider the official odds and try to predict who will win. If you have any countries to wager, the ultra-elite will call all bets.

2

Before Chicken was defeated by Ox, and her body was given a Sky Burial, she saw the matador's bloody saber and assumed that he had killed at least one other fighter, but that conclusion was a hasty one. Chicken could hardly be faulted for believing the rumors that surrounded the Natural-Born Slayer—indeed, up until that day, none had ever faced Ox in combat and survived—but his perfect killing streak had been broken just shortly before she met her death at his hands. Against his previous opponent, his saber had wounded its intended target, but he hadn't been able to make the kill.

Even though a single thrust of his blade had always been more than enough to kill, Ox took the precaution to stab Chicken in both her eyes due to the experience he'd just had. If the encounter had been enough to rattle the Natural, it would have stricken terror into the heart of an average person.

That being the case, this enemy who faced Ox and lived should have been proud at breaking the Natural's perfect record. But that wasn't the kind of person Horse was.

Horse was Horse. Now, for the first time, he had been wounded—both in body and in spirit. Anywhere and anyone he fought, he had never—literally never—received a single scratch, but now his armorlike body, the product of the technique he called Stirrup, was covered all over with saber wounds.

None had been fatal, and most were mere scrapes. None had penetrated to his bones or internal organs, and few even reached his muscles—but wounds were wounds. A good number of them even looked like they would leave scars. The thought of it left his well-earned pride as shredded as his skin.

He hadn't been able to counter Ox's attacks by any measure worth reporting, and though their match resulted in a draw, it was only because Horse hadn't died—to him, the tie felt like utter defeat.

But his betting odds hadn't languished in the middling ranks simply because of the great number of physical wounds he had. By virtue of simply having survived Ox, Horse's popularity should have risen, if anything, but his actions after the fight made for a tremendously poor impression.

Horse fled into the vault of a major bank, barricaded himself inside, and then did nothing. The man with the impenetrable defense had shut himself away to wait for an attack to come. From no possible perspective did the strategy make any sense. With the time limit imposed by the poison jewels, no great leaps of logic were needed to realize that holing up somewhere wouldn't work.

The only conclusion to be drawn from Horse's actions was that the nearly two-meter-tall warrior was afraid to face Ox again, and now, broken and demoralized, he had confined himself away from the battle. That his odds hadn't plummeted all the way to last place was a small miracle.

Of course, Horse didn't know of the odds assigned to him by the gods on high, and he cared nothing for what others thought of him—but no one found him more a disappointment than he did. Contempt and disgust might have even been better words for what he felt toward himself.

He wasn't lacking in excuses for the stalemate had he wanted to take solace in them. When he encountered Ox, Horse didn't think it was going to turn into a fight. Maybe he should have known better, but they shared something in common—both had supported Monkey's proposal in the starting room. Then, when Rabbit had raised his hand, Ox and Horse lowered theirs in unison. Even though the collapsing floor cut Monkey's alliance short, the two men could have been considered a moderate faction by virtue of showing interest in a peaceful solution, should one have existed.

When by chance he encountered Ox, Horse hoped the two could team up. With Ox's sword-fighting skills and Horse's defense combined, teaming up would have been like equipping themselves with the spear that could pierce all shields, and the shield that could block all spears—unstoppable force and immovable object working in tandem. So great would be their advantage they might have been able to shape the battle as they wished. But that didn't happen.

Horse felt ashamed—ashamed that he had let himself hope he would be so lucky. So strong was his shame that he wanted to tear out his hair. Of course, with his impenetrable defense, he couldn't have plucked a single eyelash even if he tried with all his might. His flesh had been carved with wounds even he couldn't have made.

In his present state of mind, Horse wouldn't have felt any better knowing that his judgment had been fundamentally correct—he and Ox were the moderates among the twelve fighters of the Twelfth Zodiac War. Horse was Horse, but the Natural-Born Slayer—though he brought merciless massacres to every battlefield he graced—didn't fight because he enjoyed it. If calling a professional soldier a moderate would be too much of a stretch, think of it this way: fighting was only a job to him, as opposed to Ox's polar opposites, Rabbit and Tiger, who fought in order to kill and took pleasure in combat.

Though Horse couldn't know it, Ox had an unobvious reason for forcing the fight. After the eleven combatants were separated, the muscled giant ran into Ox first. But Ox had encountered another before him—although to be precise, he didn't encounter this other fighter, because he was very careful to steer clear of the ashen-faced walking corpse belonging to the woman who used to be the Fighter of the Boar. At that point, Ox didn't know that Rabbit was the one controlling her, but he inferred from her presence that a necromanticist was among the twelve combatants.

The moment Ox reached that conclusion, finding a peaceful resolution to the Zodiac War was no longer an option for him. Instead, he decided he needed to kill as many of his opponents with his own hands as he could. A necromanticist gained dominance over those whom he killed—if Ox stood idly by, this adversary could forge an unbreakable alliance of up to eleven people. The only way Ox could prevent this outcome was to kill the other fighters before they were killed by the necromanticist. Though the moderate Ox might have allied himself with his opponents under different circumstances, killing them had become an act of mercy; it was the least he could do for them. Compared with the necromanticist defiling their corpses, a quick and painless death at the hand of the Natural-Born Slayer might deliver them more peace in the afterlife. Unlike Horse, his moderate counterpart, Ox possessed the pure talent that allowed him to make that decision.

Regardless, Horse had no way of knowing Ox's intentions, and when abruptly faced with the battle, the giant hadn't been mentally prepared. The Natural, on the other hand, having already decided to kill the other fighters, was vastly more resolute.

But excuses were only excuses. The battle had been abrupt, but Ox didn't catch him unaware or unguarded; the matador gave the proper introduction and even allowed Horse time to prepare himself before lunging with that saber. Ox's conduct had been beyond reproach, and the fight was fair.

Though thrown into disarray at first, Horse was soon fighting to kill, and the ultimate stalemate mortified him. No wonder he wanted to hide. It bears repeating that the mere act of surviving against that master saber-wielder was a spectacular feat—but that made for cold comfort when the bodybuilder's devotion to his muscles was practically religious. In a sense, Ox's attacks had pierced his defenses and inflicted critical damage to the core of who he was. Even if Horse had from now to the end of the Zodiac War, it was not an injury from which he would easily recover.

But for a man who boasted such an impenetrable defense—or rather, if that label no longer applied, then a peerlessly robust defense—to now barricade himself in a bank vault was like protecting a steel statue with a plastic case. It was nonsensical.

Withdrawing from the battle was the lowest course of action a warrior could take, but as a human, as a living being, the choice was not necessarily a bad one. Looking at it from a different perspective—from a proper distance—the notion was hard to dismiss as merely foolish—not when winning this Zodiac War required collecting the swallowed poison jewels. If just one participant vacated the field of battle, the rest would all die from the poison. The way the contest was set up, even the weakest fighter, who might have little chance at victory, possessed the real potential to make the rest die with him.

The strongest fighter, then, needed to avoid overwhelming the weakest fighters so thoroughly that the weak would abandon the contest—and in Horse's case, Ox had gone too far. Once Ox crossed that line, he needed to do everything in his power to make the kill. Maybe the natural-born warrior couldn't fathom what it felt like to not be dead but broken-spirited.

Setting aside the discussion of the nature of Ox's virtuosity for another time, when Horse lost his will to fight and barricaded himself away, he put the more likely winners, like Rabbit and Ox, in greater jeopardy. For all twelve fighters to die would be an unsatisfying end to the contest, but what reason did Horse have to give anyone a satisfying ending?

Horse wasn't even sure he'd die from the poison when the time limit ran out. That would depend upon Stirrup. If this were a role-playing game, Stirrup bestowed upon him the defense of a post-game item. If his special ability could protect him from external attacks, then maybe—just maybe—it would work against internal attacks—even poison. That could have been his advantage, just as Rabbit the necromanticist could gather a tight alliance, and Dog had neutralized the poison in his body, and Chicken's Eye of the Cormorant lifted the fog of war. If he, too, possessed some advantage tailored to the rules of the game, maybe this was it.

Of course, Horse had no proof behind this theory, and it wasn't as if he barricaded himself in the bank vault having thought through any such plan. But if all the other fighters died from their poison, and Horse alone survived, then maybe the result wouldn't count as a victory under the rules of the game, but as a living being, survival itself was a victory. As Sheep would have said, to live was to win.

Given this unexpected turn of events, the warriors who were still fiercely competing now found themselves in a precarious position. The likely winners—Ox, Rabbit, and Tiger—all possessed abilities that focused on fighting other people—none had the capability to smash through a barricade that had no entrance or exit. The only ones who had possessed that kind of pure destructive power had been Boar and her machine guns and Sheep and his grenades, but both fighters had already passed on to the next world. Barring any dark horse upsetting the contest's current trajectory, the Twelfth Zodiac War would reach an ignoble conclusion.

The worst ending, however, would be if Horse's Stirrup proved ineffective against the poison and he died like the others, only all alone in the vault.

Then a voice said, "If we don't get some light in here, I'm going to fall asleep."

A light then sprang to life and pierced the pitch-black darkness inside the vault. It seemed like magic, although the source of this light was purely technological, the exact opposite of fantasy. Though everyone walked around carrying one of the gadgets, it represented the culmination of modern technology—a smartphone. The glow of the awakened screen illuminated the vault and revealed not only the giant man slumped over, hugging his knees as he sat on the floor—but also the smartphone's owner.

He was a boy in his mid-teens—of the demographic perhaps the least surprising to own a smartphone. It was the Fighter of the Rat, though Horse only knew him as the napping kid from the high-rise.

Rat's sleepy eyes were fixed on his phone, like a commuter checking his email on the train. Without looking at Horse, he mumbled, almost as if talking in his sleep, "They say the glass they use on these smartphones is the same stuff the military uses. I heard about this guy that got shot with one in his pocket, and the phone stopped the bullet. Like an urban legend or something. You think it's true?"

Without waiting for an answer, Rat continued, "You know, when I get a new phone, I'm the type who cracks the screen on purpose, first thing. The screen gets these radial cracks, almost like a spider web. It looks kinda badass, right?"

Horse hadn't heard of anyone who broke their new phones on purpose, let alone that there was apparently a "type." Horse was the type who never even removed the protective film. One could say that he had holed himself away in the vault because he spent his life fearing such scrapes, and that touches upon a serious, broader social issue, but this was no time for a therapy session. A more pressing question was at hand—how had the boy gotten inside?

Answering the unasked question, Rat said, "Oh, don't worry about that. The thing about rats is, they always find their way in through even the smallest cracks."

A crack? When Horse had entered the bank vault, he broke the lock behind him. The vault door was already built to keep intruders out, and he had enhanced the bulwark even further with a hastily constructed barricade of the heaviest objects he could find. Horse couldn't guarantee that, given infinite time to search, an invader would never find a way through, but he was certain he hadn't left any gap or any crack that could have been found and exploited so quickly.

Yet here the boy was.

"I am Nezumi, the Fighter of the Rat. I kill inexorably."

Rat tossed out his introduction without even looking up from his smartphone. There was nothing of the fighter left in Horse, but he responded by rote.

"I am Uuma, the Fighter of the Horse. I kill in silence."

Here he was calling himself a fighter when he didn't even feel he deserved to be called the head of the Sōma clan. Until now, all he had felt was fear; for the first time, he felt self-loathing.

If Rat noticed, he didn't show it. "Okay," he said, eyes still glued to the glowing screen. The boy gave no indication that he was going to attack. From the battle's start, he hadn't once shown any interest in fighting. Since Horse was in no condition to fight, he owed his life to the boy's apathy.

But Horse still had questions he would have liked to ask, like, "How did you get in here?" or similarly, "Why did you come in here?"

Unprompted, Rat said, "Oh, I just needed kind of an emergency shelter. Like a panic room, right? This Snake guy is chasing me. Well, I say Snake guy, but he's really a corpse. I was supposed to be chasing him, but things happened. It's like I'm being surrounded by the coils of a boa constrictor. Well he is Snake, eh?"

Horse didn't know what the boy was talking about. Rat certainly didn't seem to want to stop and explain either—it felt like he was talking to himself, if anything. A fighter who didn't talk and a fighter who talked to himself, together in a locked room—just where was this going?

"Say, you were on board with Monkey's peace proposal, weren't you? Since you're letting me crash here, I'll let you know—that all went up in smoke. No Monkey, no peace. And Monkey got herself killed. That pacifist was at the heart of whatever plan she was cooking up, so that's finished now. You know, I shouldn't speak ill of the dead, but she was a real loser. It's like, what good does all that talk about peace do when you're killed? She never even told anyone what her plan was. Now it's gone with her. You ask me, I think she might have just been making it up. She saw negotiating cease-fires as her heroic duty, after all. So maybe the first step was just to say anything she could say to stop the fighting, and then everyone could think of a solution together, or something like that. Sounds believable to me. No matter how prim and proper a front she put on, a hero would still pull a trick like that for the right cause. Don't underestimate her hollow words, right?"

These half-mumbled ramblings weren't enough to give Horse a good picture of what had happened outside, but he caught the part about a top competitor being killed. Who had killed her? Was it Ox with his saber?

"I just don't get it," Rat said. "Just how important is peace anyway? If everyone just stays on the defense, like you're doing, the world will stop changing, won't it? Audacity and mischief, that's what brings change and evolution. A world that's gone still is no different than a world that's been wiped out. Just like how you're the same as dead right now."

Horse didn't know what the kid was talking about. He didn't want to know either.

"Being alive without taking action is the same as being dead. Compared to that, those corpses under that freakish rabbit's control seem more alive. Say, you don't know where that Sheep geezer is, do you?"

Sheep...geezer? Did he mean that old man who asked about his use of explosives? Horse had a vague recollection of the man, but why did this boy want to know his whereabouts?

"Ah, you don't know," Rat said. "That's fine. Well, don't worry about it. All right, I'd better get going. Hiding away in a place like this would be too demoralizing—or like being a horse with a busted leg, waiting to get shot. Bye then."

The boy put his phone to sleep as if he'd finished replying to his mail. The vault plunged back into total darkness, and the boy seemed to have gone.

Then Rat said one last thing. "That Snake guy might come here looking for me. I think you should escape too. At least, you should do something, anything—that is, if you're still alive. If you want to keep living."

By the time Horse's eyes adjusted to the dark, the boy really had left. Rat's parting commentary was as arrogant as his invasion of Horse's sanctum, but the fact was they were in the midst of a battle. The broken-spirited fighter should have been thankful that Rat had spared his life. He wondered if maybe he should take the child's advice. If he simply blamed Rat for bringing danger to this place, then Horse would be the arrogant one.

But where could Horse run? Outside was Ox, the Natural-Born Slayer. However dangerous remaining in the vault might have been, going out there was far worse.

The mystery of how Rat had slipped past the barricade remained, but Snake—or was it Snake's corpse—would surely be incapable of the same feat. Even if Horse took Rat's warning in earnest, remaining barricaded in the safety of the vault still seemed the best course of action. As long as he was safe, he needed nothing else.

Rat's words echoed in Horse's mind. "A world that's gone still is no different than a world that's been wiped out. Being alive without taking action is the same as being dead." For some reason, he couldn't shake them. Again and again, the phrases repeated, dizzying his thoughts.

They were just the casual teasing of some kid who knew nothing about how the world worked. They were just one-sided ramblings which Horse had no need to take seriously. But he couldn't get them out of his mind.

To shelter, to withdraw, to do nothing; to no longer need to fight should have been the easiest thing in the world, but instead it felt stifling—so oppressive, so suffocating, Horse could hardly breathe.

He could hardly breathe.

Suddenly, Horse realized it wasn't the boy's words that were making him feel this way, but by the time he stood, the vault was already filled with smoke, the shadows taken over by black clouds. Something was burning.

Not something. Everything.

The entire vault was burning. The temperature was rising with no end in sight, and the air carried an acrid stench so foul and so powerful it almost made Horse faint.

But the vault wasn't just burning.

It had been set on fire.

Had someone judged his barricade too strong to be destroyed and decided to burn it? What, to melt it away? It made no sense. Horse's defensive ability, Stirrup, would not be so easily damaged, even from the heat of a blaze.

But even though Stirrup was resilient against damage inflicted upon him, it was not so robust against damage resulting from something being taken away. Human life required oxygen, and so did fire; if the latter consumed all the oxygen, then the fate of the former was certain.

Confronted by this primitive, primal force—this chemical action—the silent warrior (or rather, former warrior), who sought survival through inaction, released a final cry that might have been a whinny.

3

The headless corpse stood before the burned-out husk of the bank. He had set fire to the vault, barricade and all—or rather, it wasn't he who had done it. Yes, the liquid flames had been spewed by the flamethrower strapped to his back, the one he had worn as the Fighter of the Snake before his head was taken from him, but his actions after his death were under the necromanticist's command.

His current command was to pursue Rat, and Snake had only set fire to the vault as part of the chase. Though he had no head with which to see or speak, he sensed that he had failed to finish the boy off. He didn't linger over the building's smoldering remains; he simply turned his back, and tenacious as his namesake, he pursued his prey.

In this way, Horse, the defensive giant, succeeded in escaping the battle—by being defeated without a fight.

RABBIT VS. ~~HORSE~~
END OF THE 6ᵀᴴ BATTLE

THE SEVENTH BATTLE

"The head of a dragon, but the tail of only a snake."
(First Round)

**TATSUMI
BROTHER,
THE YOUNGER;
THE FIGHTER
OF THE SNAKE**

"I wish for money."

REAL NAME: **Takeyasu TSUMITA**
BORN: **October 10 (officially)**
HEIGHT: **164 cm**
WEIGHT: **58 kg**

Takeyasu is a young warrior who fights alongside his elder twin brother. Such fiercely idiosyncratic fighters rarely band together on the battlefield, but Dragon and Snake provide a legendary exception. Their superiority in battle goes without saying; though they are only the most recent of a long line of Tatsumi Brothers, they work together better than any in history.

The younger brother favors weapons of flame in battle, and he has a reputation for starting fires so devastating that the bodies of his enemies can't be told apart from one another. He often claims that without the outlet his mercenary career provides him, he would have been a serial arsonist. He is undoubtedly a most dangerous man.

He calls the flamethrower he wears on his back *Hitokage*, written with the *kanji* for "person" and "shadow"—the implication being that he will burn people until not even their shadows are left. That the name shares the same pronunciation as the word for "salamander" is intentional.

At home, he raises a wide variety of reptiles. He publishes an anonymous blog, which is incredibly popular among fellow enthusiasts, about his experiences raising the creatures. Whenever a precious pet passes away, he grills the reptile and eats it. Unlike the battlefield, where he doesn't give any thought to those he kills, when it comes to his pets, he looks after them all the way to the end.

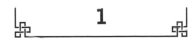

1

Five challengers remained in this, the Twelfth Zodiac War. In zodiac order, they were: Rat, Ox, Tiger, Rabbit, and Dragon. To recap their accomplishments, Rabbit had killed Snake, Boar, Monkey, and Horse; while Ox and Tiger killed Chicken and Sheep respectively. Rat had not defeated anyone, and Dragon had not yet been in a fight. That said, the Zodiac War was not a contest of who could kill the most people, nor was it at all relevant who among the fighters was the strongest. In some cases, depending on the rules and the course of events, a person might claim victory without ever fighting any opponents.

Based on all present knowledge, one fighter—Rabbit, the only to form a lasting team—held an overwhelming advantage over his enemies. Not only had he successfully formed an alliance, his corpses acted as a monolithic unit over which he held absolute command. He had lost the former Fighter of the Boar to a ravenous flock of birds, but his remaining forces continued to pose a considerable threat to the other fighters—and now that fewer than half the combatants remained, Rabbit and his minions were a greater danger than ever.

The second half of the Twelfth Zodiac War would now hinge upon the eradication of Team Rabbit. In theory, the simplest solution would have been for the other four fighters to join forces, if only temporarily, and fight as one team against another. That idea, however, was doomed to remain a fantasy. The fighter most capable of building an alliance was Monkey—who now belonged to Rabbit—and of the remaining living challengers, Dragon—who had not yet battled any opponent, and whose movements remained a mystery—was unlikely to cooperate. In all of Dragon's experience on the battlefield—and off it, in his daily life—he had never worked alongside anyone except his little brother.

At present, the surviving fighters had no practical course of action to thwart Usagi, the Fighter of Rabbit, and his corpse army.

2

"I am Tatsumi the Elder, the Fighter of the Dragon. I kill for the money."

"I am Tatsumi the Younger, the Fighter of the Snake. I kill for the money."

The brothers would never again stand shoulder to shoulder, striking an intrepid pose, and announce themselves in unison. For one thing, the younger brother's vocal chords had been severed in two. Unable to hear, smell, or speak, his headless corpse wandered the ghost town that served as the Zodiac War's battlegrounds. The roaming dead seemed a perfect fit for an abandoned city, but this corpse wasn't simply walking at random.

He walked with a purpose—not his own, as he possessed no consciousness, but a purpose nonetheless. His superior had assigned him a command as relentlessly unfeeling as the corpse itself—kill the Fighter of the Rat.

He didn't have to understand whom it was he pursued. Nothing mattered to him anymore. Without a consciousness, he couldn't think; without thought, he couldn't make any decisions; without making a decision, he couldn't stop. The corpse kept on walking and kept on moving.

That he couldn't see or hear didn't matter either. Much like the slithering reptiles with which Snake shared affinity, the fighter's feet detected minute vibrations in the ground that allowed him to sense and react to his surroundings—although to be clear, he was dead, so he didn't sense anything. He merely reacted to the stimuli, like a dissected frog hooked up to electrodes, each jolt spurring its legs into motion.

The detailed mechanics aside, Snake's unique ability— Earth's Guidance—served as a kind of sonar that would lead him to Rat wherever the youth fled and hid—even if the hiding place was, for example, a bank vault. But a zombie was still a zombie, and Snake didn't move with great speed, but because he had no conscious self, he would never give up his tireless pursuit, not until his legs rotted and snapped—and possibly not even then.

Meanwhile, Rabbit kept Snake's head and took it with him to a new location. Rabbit had made excellent use of the severed head in his fight against Monkey, and he seemed to have another use for it in mind now.

That brings up a difficult question that once raised may never be settled—what constitutes a person? Which portion of the human body is the man? When Snake's head was removed from his body, in what part did his essence dwell? His mind was in his head, but his heart was in his chest; his hands were what used tools, his legs were what walked.

To take the question a step further, at what point could a person be said to have died? Even when a person's heart stops, if their heart can be restarted within five minutes, their brain might not be affected. If a person's brain stops functioning, modern medical science can keep their body alive. What about judging by volume? The human liver accounts for a miniscule portion of the body, but remove it, and that person would have a lot of trouble staying alive. A haircut doesn't hurt at all, but a person's hair still contains their unique DNA.

When children lose their baby teeth, can those teeth be considered separate lives? What about a corpse? Even a body declared dead, with its pupils dilated, still retains warmth for a time. Is that warmth entirely separate from life?

As a question of bioethics, the subject may never be settled, but fortunately for Rabbit and Snake, the necromanticist had no ethical code, and the corpse no consciousness—neither found themselves troubled by the matter. By Rabbit's unfeeling orders—no lingering warmth to be found in his machinations—Snake, the headless corpse, would prowl the abandoned streets until he caught the escaped rat.

Someone hiccupped.

With footsteps even more faltering than those of the corpse, a drunk woman moved into his path.

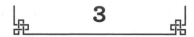

3

The Zodiac War had progressed beyond the initial standoff phase—where the fighters felt out the situation and each other. Partly, this was due to the handful of fights that had already broken out here and there, but the bank fire started by Snake became the deciding factor. The blaze spread across a far wider area than just the vault itself, with plenty of combustible material to keep the fire burning for quite some time.

A giant column of smoke rose like a beacon above the abandoned city and commanded the attention of the remaining combatants. Its message was clear: like it or not, the battle was not merely half over—it was entering its endgame.

Neither was the message lost on the drunken Tiger. Following the smoke plume, she staggered there from the park on tottering legs. Skunk drunk and wearing next to nothing, the young woman made for a repulsive sight, but Snake had no reaction. The repugnance he might have once felt toward her was nowhere to be found in him.

The corpse didn't need to feel anything; he simply mechanically followed Rabbit's instructions: to kill any warriors who stood in the way of his search for Rat. That his opponent was a young woman, or a drunk, didn't concern him—nothing did.

Tiger growled at him, then slurred, "Huh? What's with you? Did your head fall off somewhere?"

She regarded the zombie with a bewildered tilt of her head—tilting so far that hers too might have been about to fall off. Tiger was as yet unaware that a necromanticist was among the fighters, and stumbling across a roaming, headless corpse should have come as an extreme shock to the drunken woman, but that was the extent of her reaction—either because her blood wasn't doing a good job of reaching her brain, or the alcohol was doing too good a one.

"Wait, I remember you," she said. "You're that guy with that badass weapon on your back." Then she laughed and pointed a mocking finger at him. "You got killed before we even started."

The insult, of course, didn't anger him. Had he still been alive, he would have likely been enraged—he had despised this kind of woman before his death—but he had no likes or dislikes now; no prejudice and no disdain.

Seeing that he wasn't going to respond, she continued, "Well then, what am I going to do with you? This is complicated. I'm not good with complicated."

She had no idea what to make of this walking corpse—either she didn't know anything about necromanticists, or she was too drunk to remember.

Then Snake attacked.

"Whoa!" she said, performing a backflip out of Hitokage's blast of flame. In her state, whether she had easily or only barely evaded the liquid fire was hard to guess, but either way, she failed to stick the landing, instead crashing flat on her stomach in a sloppy heap.

Sensing the vibration from her impact, Snake released another burst of fire at her. But the drunk, more herself on the ground than on her feet, skillfully rolled and dodged the merciless attack.

"This isn't the circus," she said, distancing herself from the corpse. "I'm not jumping through fire for you."

Then the wielder of the Drunken Fist got on all fours, as she had done when she faced off against Sheep in the park, and let out a long, menacing growl. Tiger was more savage beast than fighter, but the corpse couldn't be intimidated.

Instead, like a machine stuck in a perpetually looping routine, the zombie simply adjusted the aim of his flamethrower's nozzle to keep it trained on her.

She clicked her tongue. Still trying to get a rise out of him, she said, "What drunks need are cold showers, not hot ones. Anyway, my throat's parched enough as it is without you drying it up any more. Besides, what I drank burned enough on the way down already."

Nothing. He aimed his flamethrower, ready to unleash fire hot enough to melt the asphalt around her. Then, as he was about to squeeze the trigger—

"I am Tora, the Fighter of the Tiger. I kill with drunken power."

Before he could finish squeezing the trigger, his arm was gone. The corpse felt no pain when her sharp claws ripped off his limb, nor did the trauma send him into shock. He didn't try to go after it either.

But when a weight suddenly lifted from his back, even the corpse reacted. She had relieved him of not only his right arm but his flamethrower as well.

This time, the drunk woman made the landing, though in a three-point stance. In one hand, she had the flamethrower and its tank. "What's in this anyway? Alcohol, isn't it? Well, it's mine now."

She unscrewed the tank's cap and happily chugged its contents. The liquid inside was of course not alcohol, but it burned going down all the same. Within moments, she'd drained the flamethrower's many gallons of fuel as if performing a magic trick. She smacked her lips and tossed the weapon back to him, saying, "All done."

Snake let the flamethrower clatter onto the ground. The faceless corpse oriented toward her and took a different fighting stance than before.

Her eyes widened. Drunk as she was, she still recognized that stance. Despite his missing arm, the stance remained familiar to those who knew it—and Tiger knew it.

She grinned with delight. "Hey, that's snake style! Nice. *Nice.* Snake boxing versus drunken boxing—kind of old school, huh?"

Then the next instant, her mood soured. Severe mood swings were a drunk's staple, but she took it to the extreme, growling and baring her teeth in rage.

"What the hell? You're just a corpse, aren't you? Some goddamn corpse under someone else's control?"

She'd come to the realization perhaps a bit late—but she'd noticed something that would have clued in anyone no matter how drunk or how ignorant of necromanticism.

Not a single drop of blood flowed from the arm's stump.

Several hours had passed since Rabbit had killed the younger twin. Rigor mortis was beginning to set in—Snake's movements had begun to slow, and the blood inside him had completely coagulated. This development had little effect on the zombie, whose movements were already sluggish to begin with, but it mattered to Tiger.

The woman, whose Drunken Fist was more powerfully charged by blood than by alcohol, said, "That's it, I've had enough. This is stupid. My blades," she said, brandishing her claws, "are thirsty."

Tiger released her fighting stance and got to her feet. Whatever her particular grievance, the woman losing interest in the fight was—from a broader point of view—entirely reasonable. Setting aside her possibly fetishistic desire to get drunk on blood, from her position as one of the few remaining fighters, battling Snake at this point would be of limited benefit. The younger twin had been killed before the Zodiac War began; having never swallowed the poison jewel required for victory, he didn't possess one for her to take. Fighting him now, even assuming she would win, would bring her nothing of measure.

Killing him would fulfill some strategic purpose in reducing Team Rabbit's strength, but she had no particular need to do that here and now. If her goal was to be the ultimate winner, then she could leave the corpse for a rival to fight—or, looking at it from another angle, force a rival or rivals into fighting the monster. To do so risked Rabbit gaining yet another follower, but that outcome wasn't guaranteed. Also possible was the ideal result—that her rival and the corpse killed each other. If she instead chose to fight, the worst outcome was the corpse somehow getting the upper hand on her. Tiger had no compelling reason to risk her life by fighting Snake.

Whether or not Tiger, in her drunken haze, had performed such an analysis of the scenario, the fact remained that she had lost all desire to fight the corpse. And if she didn't want to, she wouldn't, instead choosing to back down from the standoff. The decision was one of incredible arrogance, but the dead Tatsumi brother didn't respond.

But a response was required of him. Her insolent, one-sided withdrawal faced him with an internal conflict he struggled to resolve.

The conflict didn't stem from any emotional source such as anger or indignation. He was, after all, a corpse, and her lack of consideration for him was normal, in a sense. He didn't feel slighted, nor did he have the capacity to—but his instructions compelled him to follow two separate and incompatible actions: to pursue the leaving woman, and to let her go. No matter how loyal the corpse was to the necromanticist, no matter that he would never betray his only friend, a contradiction in his orders made following them impossible—just as an error in programming code created bugs in a program.

If Rabbit told him to fly, Snake didn't have the capacity to obey. If Rabbit told him to turn left and right at the same time, Snake couldn't do that either—well, seeing how he was a dead body, he probably could have torn himself in two and followed the command, but that was beside the point, which was this: the younger twin had been ordered to seek, fight, and kill his target—Nezumi, the Fighter of the Rat—and to kill any other fighter who tried to stop him.

On the surface, this appeared an entirely reasonable command capable of covering a wide range of circumstances. Besides, instructions much more complicated than that would have been more than an unthinking zombie could handle. But the orders left one question unresolved—how should he deal with a fighter who didn't try to stop him?

Faced with the puzzling behavior of the fickle drunk, who first stood in his path but then turned away on a whim, the zombie didn't seem to have permission to attack her, and so he didn't know what to do. Even the dead man could recognize he shouldn't let Tiger get away, but without the proper instruction, he couldn't. Instead, he froze.

This lasted only a brief moment. The indecision did not present an infinite loop. The conflict would resolve itself as soon as she left his sight, and even if she didn't, the problem was not so complex as to be insurmountable. In the end, he would have likely concluded that his primary directive was to find Rat, and if forced to choose between pursuing him or Tiger, the corpse would choose Rat.

Snake didn't know that the necromanticist hadn't actually placed that much importance behind the order. Rabbit had simply intended to use the headless corpse to lure away an interloper from interfering with his true goal—to make Monkey his follower. Rabbit just hadn't bothered to overwrite the command. The necromanticist felt no particular attachment toward the instructions, and—though he probably hadn't forgotten about them entirely—he would hardly think twice before replacing them, should another need for the zombie arise.

And so, dutifully following orders that only still existed by default, the younger twin turned his attention from the departing Tiger and back onto Rat, when—

"I am Ushii, the Fighter of the Ox. I just kill."

The long, slender blade of Ox's saber struck the corpse.

4

This time, Snake's left arm went flying. Unlike his right arm, which was violently torn off, this was done with a perfect surgical slice, but as before, no spurting blood accompanied the amputation. The corpse lost its balance and keeled over. Now the body was without a head and both arms, but he still didn't die. Well, he *was* dead, technically, but not destroyed. Tottering, he tried to stand on his legs.

The melancholic swordfighter, Ox, looked down at the corpse in silence, waiting for the body to stand. This wasn't out of some fighter's code of conduct, but rather out of necessary caution toward his undead adversary. Ox knew how a living opponent would react to his attacks, but the zombie's unconventional movements couldn't be predicted. The swordfighter's working theory was that if stabbing the corpse wouldn't stop it, then he would keep cutting parts off until the corpse could no longer move.

Ox usually targeted a vital organ and a quick kill, but when he lopped off the zombie's arm, it wasn't because he missed, nor was he holding back. If Snake managed to stand back up, Ox would cut off his legs next. No matter the necromanticist's powers, no matter the state of Snake's undeath, a zombie physically incapable of movement was effectively the same as a plain dead body.

Unlike Tiger, Ox had a heightened fighter's awareness—when he had seen Boar's shambling corpse, the swordfighter had stayed away from the obvious trap, but when the opportunity was right, he didn't let the minutiae of risk and reward stop him. He just killed.

"No," Ox said, "please wait a moment. There's no need to rush, now, is there?"

But Ox wasn't talking to Snake's corpse, which continued its vain struggle to rise. If Monkey had been a believer in peace, then Ox was a devout pragmatist. Talking to a corpse would have been a solely self-serving act with no discernible useful purpose. Rather, he was addressing Tiger, who had come growling back to the scene.

Hardly had she announced her departure before she reappeared—and she came on all fours, ready for battle. She must have sensed the fight and doubled back. Despite her drunkenness—or possibly because of it—she keenly sensed the strangest things. Ox's masterful saber slice hadn't made the slightest noise, but maybe she'd heard the sound the arm made when it plopped to the ground—or maybe the blood-drunk beast caught the scent of the blood-soaked swordsman.

The crawling beast and the gloomy swordfighter stood on either side of the writhing corpse in a bizarre three-way stand-off. This wasn't the stand-off of legend between snake, frog, and slug, but rather Snake, Tiger, and Ox—and it didn't look like Tiger was going to wait her turn.

"You can't wait?" Ox said. "I think it's more important I take care of this corpse first. Worry not, I promise I'll make sure to kill you so that you'll never be turned into a wretched zombie like him." He paused, then added, "If I'm not mistaken, you're the Fighter of the Tiger, yes?"

"Yeah, I am." Compared to when she had confronted the corpse, she was not so glib now. Like the kind of drunk who talked less the more she drank, Tiger spent few words as she glared at Ox. But she did say, "And you're Ox, right? Ushii, the Natural-Born Slayer?"

She made it sound like she knew him from more than just his reputation. "That's right," Ox said. "You seem to know me—have we met somewhere before?"

Rather than answer, Tiger scraped at the pavement as if sharpening her claws. She growled with even deeper ferocity than when she'd realized Snake—who continued to struggle between them—was a corpse whose blood had gone too thick to drink.

Ox sighed. "It seems like I've earned your enmity somewhere along the way. Perhaps I killed your parents?"

He said that as if it were a common occurrence for him, then reoriented the tip of his saber from Snake to Tiger. The Natural-Born Slayer seemed to have decided to deal with her before the younger twin's corpse managed to stand—and that the change of order posed no major upset.

The two favored winners announced themselves at the same time.

"I am Ushii, the Fighter of the Ox—"

"I am Tora, the Fighter of the Tiger—"

Only they were interrupted. In all their time in battle, no one had ever had the audacity to interrupt either Ox, or even Tiger, in such a manner.

Snake's roughly ripped-off right arm and his cleanly severed left arm leaped onto Tiger's and Ox's throats and clamped down tight.

The arms squeezed the necks of their transgressors as if to snap their vertebrae rather than simply choke them. Tiger growled and Ox grunted.

Where does a person begin and end? Where does a life begin and end? The two arms attempted to crush any such questions along with the necks of the two fighters.

The corpse was still not yet standing.

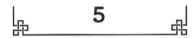

5

From above, a figure watched the chaotic battle between Ox, Tiger, and the dead body and the two dead arms. Not the Eye of the Cormorant, this watcher's measured gaze came from somewhere higher than birds could fly, and higher still, almost in the stratosphere. He was less witnessing the battle than he was watching over an underachieving little brother who was trying to do his best.

This watcher, who flew through the sky with more freedom than even the birds, was the fighter who represented the only mythical creature in the Zodiac—the Dragon.

END OF THE 7ᵀᴴ BATTLE

THE EIGHTH BATTLE

"The head of a dragon, but the tail of only a snake."
(Second Round)

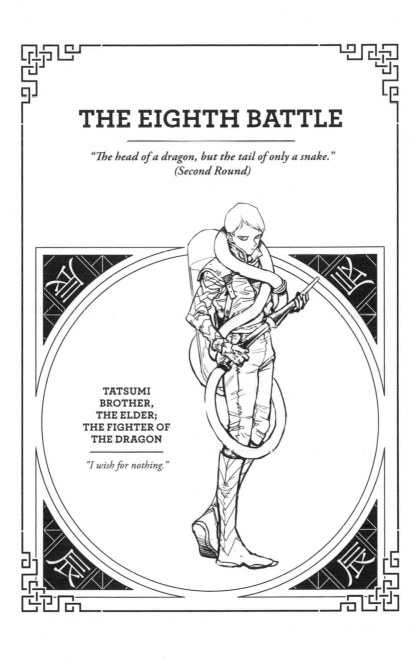

**TATSUMI
BROTHER,
THE ELDER;
THE FIGHTER OF
THE DRAGON**

"I wish for nothing."

REAL NAME: Nagayuki TSUMITA
BORN: November 11 (officially)
HEIGHT: 164 cm
WEIGHT: 58 kg

Nagayuki fights alongside his younger twin brother, but as the elder, he takes the role of the leader. The two are physically identical in every way, and the only reliable way to tell the twins apart is that Nagayuki refers to himself with the brash honorific *"Ore-sama."* Anyone who knows this fact has no trouble discerning which brother is which, but since they don't typically try to pass as one another, this doesn't bother them.

As fighters, the Tatsumi brothers don't particularly adhere to any code; as long as an agreement over payment can be reached, they will fight for any country, on any scale, in any war. Their conduct, often unbefitting warriors of the twelve houses, has frequently earned them various punishments, but they show no signs of reforming.

The following is a defense statement Nagayuki made while covering for his younger brother in a Hearing of Censure: "Even when the wealthy are heavily taxed, those taxes are ultimately used for their own benefit. We're just redirecting that money to more proper ends."

The brothers disgrace their profession through their heinous deeds, but the money they sweep up from the wealthy class they pour into philanthropic endeavors. They might use blood money earned through a mass slaughter to save a single child in dire need. This isn't because they're some form of chivalrous thieves or people of virtue, or are good deep down, or run hot and cold like *tsundere* or anything like that. They simply find a kind of decadent amusement in blowing through the money earned through bad deeds on righteous purposes. They always remain mindful of not allowing their good deeds to change them into good people.

His icethrower, *Yuki onna*, is the complement to his brother's flamethrower, Hitokage, and its tank is filled with liquid hydrogen. Though he may not say it, he considers his weapon harder to use than his younger brother's.

Let us take this moment to sort out how many poison jewels were in each fighter's possession at this point of the Twelfth Zodiac War—though keep in mind this will serve only as a snapshot of the contest's current state.

With the spectacle of all the killings, it could be easy to forget that the winner would be the fighter who held all twelve poison jewels—including the one he or she swallowed.

Rabbit remained in the lead by having secured three jewels in addition to his own: those of Boar, whom he skewered; Monkey, whose lungs he'd collapsed; and Horse, who suffocated in Snake's fire. Though the necromanticist hadn't killed Horse himself, he possessed a near comprehensive awareness of his minions' actions and was able to claim the jewel. Excavating the vault's burned-down remains took some effort, and cutting open Horse's Stirrup to retrieve the prize necessitated creative thinking, but Monkey's mountain magic came in handy there.

Rabbit's allies worked as a cohesive unit, with each member's strengths complementing the others' deficiencies. Their biggest missing asset was common sense, but seeing how none of the combatants—whether dead, alive, or undead—possessed that trait, Team Rabbit would have to go without.

Ox held the second highest number of jewels. He had killed only Chicken so far, but she had already claimed Dog's jewel, which brought Ox's count to three. Tiger held two— her own and Sheep's.

Even the drunk hadn't forgotten her part in the Zodiac War—although her altered state kept her from questioning why she had found the prize in his pocket and nothing in his stomach. Regardless, she held two jewels.

You may think that left Rat and Dragon on the bottom, with only their own jewels. But that would be forgetting that Dragon had used his relationship to Snake to claim an extra jewel, after Rabbit killed his brother before the contest began. Because of this, Rat was alone in last place, and Dragon was tied with Tiger.

Claiming his dead brother's jewel might sound like nothing more than an underhanded ploy by an unscrupulous man, but the action hadn't been without risk. Some of his opponents viewed it as the act of a coward, or worse: a fool. Nothing good would come from that sort of attention. At its core, this Zodiac War was about taking and stealing each other's jewels. Anyone who started the game with the jewels of two participants became an enticing target from a cost-performance perspective. That he would become a target was as plain as day.

Dragon had put himself in the crosshairs—and yet, the elder twin had come this far without a single fight.

If you think about it, that was very strange—highly disconcerting even. Now that the contest was approaching the endgame, his initial bounty no longer stood out from the pack, but at least in the early stages, he should have been a likely target. And yet he hadn't fought Rat or Ox or Tiger or Rabbit or Horse or Sheep or Monkey or Chicken or Dog or Boar.

No matter how much he tried to shun fighting, confrontations were not typically so easily avoided. Take the pacifist,

Monkey, who was forced into a situation where even she had no choice but to fight. And even Rat—who held the least number of jewels—chanced across Monkey, stumbled into Chicken, got chased by Snake's corpse, and talked to Horse in the bank vault. Despite all the encounters that arose between the gladiators, not one fighter had seen Dragon after they scattered at the start.

Did he do such a superior job of hiding during the initial deadlock—so much so that he remained hidden from even the Eye of the Cormorant and the necromanticist's search? The idea seemed farfetched, but he was, in fact, somewhere completely out of sight.

From the moment the fighting broke out, the elder Tatsumi brother took to the skies—higher than the skies even—where no one could see him.

He wasn't exactly in hiding but was openly surveying those beneath him with his arms crossed. This was his special ability, the Heavens' Holding. Whatever bird's-eye view Chicken's Eye of the Cormorant offered of the ground below, that downward gaze could never have seen Dragon circling on high like an ancient pterosaur. Dragons were fantastical creatures that lived in the skies; always the watchers and never the watched.

Even now Dragon observed the battle in the ghost city far below, between Ox and Tiger, and Snake, his dead brother. *He's certainly being put to good use,* Dragon thought. *First immolating Horse, then strangling Ox and Tiger at the same time— he would never have been able to pull off such an extraordinary performance when he was alive. But...*

Dragon's expression was not the same glib face he'd worn for the benefit of the other warriors at the start but one of absolute composure that could have belonged to a solemn man. The brothers had always put on an exaggerated front of being two young jokers—they cared not whether others understood them, preferring instead to keep their true selves to themselves, even if it meant looking worse than they really were—and when Dragon's younger brother was killed before his very eyes, he maintained the act and successfully claimed his brother's jewel.

The real Dragon possessed a surprisingly calm nature, along with the patience to remain in wait above the skies for hours on end, and a superior intellect, which he put to work analyzing his brother's battle—or rather, his brother's corpse's battle. No matter how astonishing his brother's efforts were, Dragon had observed countless battlefields in this manner, and the experienced aficionado of war was not simply gawking.

But this attempt won't be enough to take down fighters of Ox's and Tiger's measure. So then, what does that mean for me? Dragon had thought he'd remain there as the veritable watcher from on high for as long as possible. *But if I see a chance to eliminate Tiger, and especially Ox, I'd better not let that opportunity escape.*

2

All was silent but for Tiger's fruitless growls. She desperately clawed at the zombie arm to somehow pry it from her throat, but Snake's fingers constricted the muscles at the base of her neck and restricted her strength. Her Drunken Fist was of no use here—she couldn't punch the enemy who strangled her when his body was writhing on the ground some distance away.

Ox didn't growl, but he shared the same dilemma. He couldn't stab Snake's hand when it was firmly against his throat. No matter how superior his natural skill with the saber, if he struck from that angle he risked cutting his own neck.

With artful skill, he'd cut down every foe he'd faced, but he'd never anticipated fighting a severed arm—and one with such incredible strength. Its power was inhuman—even considering it had once belonged to a warrior. Not even the giant, Horse, had likely possessed such a grip. Was the arm so strong because it was not alive, but dead and under Rabbit's control? Ox had heard a theory that humans didn't ordinarily have the ability to utilize their full strength—that some psychological safeguard acted as a limiter—but remove that safeguard and people could utilize one hundred percent of their latent abilities. Perhaps being dead removed that safeguard—but even still, the arm's strength was incredible.

As Ox struggled for breath, even a warrior of a thousand seas and a thousand mountains wouldn't realize the answer— that this was part of who Snake was. In order to make their meals easier to swallow, snakes coiled themselves around their prey and squeezed hard enough to shatter bone. The act came naturally to the younger twin's arm.

Tiger's growls weakened, and she began to gurgle and froth at the mouth. She remained conscious—for now—but it was only a matter of time.

Ox called out to her as loudly as he could, which wasn't very much. "Tiger, can you still hear me?"

She grunted and glared his way. When she spoke, her voice dripped with venom, and some of the life had come back into it. "What do you want? I don't remember saying you could talk to me."

Ox gave her a grin, if a slight and melancholic one. "I realized why you hate me. I want you to know that I know that when I ask you this favor."

"You want to ask me a favor? How about you shut the hell up before you kill my buzz?"

"I'm not trying to upset you. I'm only asking for a temporary—*a temporary*—alliance, just to get us out of this bind. Team play is a fundamental part of a battle royale, right?"

Tiger growled at his offer, and her eyes flashed with ferocious intensity.

But Ox continued. "I promise you, as soon as we're out of this scrape, we will fight in the manner and conditions of your choosing. It won't be about the Zodiac War. It will be you and me. All right? You won't have to challenge me to a fight. This is me challenging you."

A flash of stunned surprise sobered her expression. No matter the source of her rage, anyone who knew of Ushii the Fighter of the Ox understood the weight of the solitary soldier's offer. Coming from him, requesting to join forces would have been surprising enough, and then on top of that came a demand for a duel.

This time, Tiger's growl was more hesitant, but her words carried the urgency of someone about to expend her last mental and physical strength. "A-all right. If that's how it is. So what do I do?"

"You don't have to do anything—just as long as you keep those bubbles coming."

No matter how hard Snake's hand squeezed his throat, Ox had retained his grip on his saber, which he now hurled toward Tiger with all his might. But the blade didn't hit her—nor did it hit the zombie's other arm around her neck. Instead, as if the struggle for breath and consciousness had made Ox's grip slip and turned his aim astray, the saber dropped short and scraped roughly across the pavement, kicking up a trail of sparks.

Tiger, who had nearly blacked out for the second time, was suddenly completely alert—but so would anyone be when they were enveloped by flames. Thrown into confusion, the woman dropped to the ground.

To Ox, the flames came not as a surprise but as the obvious effect of the sparks he'd intended to create. He'd seen the froth coming from her mouth—and beyond that, he'd smelled the stench of alcohol that permeated her body—and he understood that one source of ignition was all that separated her from immolation. The Drunken Fist had practically drowned herself in sake and had even guzzled a tank of flamethrower fuel. Every part of her was flammable, up to and including the froth that bubbled up with each gasping breath.

She roared as she tossed away her burning jacket and rolled on the ground. Discarding the garment would have been the right course of action, were this a typical fire that spread from the clothes to the wearer, but unfortunately, she and not her clothes was the fire's fuel source. Roll as she might, the flames stubbornly burned on.

Keeping one eye on the woman, Ox scooped up her still-burning jacket in his bare hands, and, flourishing it like a matador's *muleta*, he wrapped it around the severed arm at his neck. The heat nearly proved too much for him to bear, but he kept on wrapping, when suddenly, the arm's bone-crushing strength went slack.

This time, the arm was truly dead.

Ox said, "Maybe cremation was all it needed to rest in peace."

Ox tore the arm from his throat and tossed it to the street. Then he fell to his knees, coughing and gasping for air. Even for the natural-born fighter, the outcome had nearly been fatal. If any other proof was needed, one needed only to look to his throat, where the deep impressions left by Snake's fingers remained. Ox's skin was not only bruised but ruptured into bloody trails.

Once reanimated, the necromanticist's corpses never stopped—chop them up or cut them apart and the pieces kept moving. But in a few exceptional cases, they had been stopped with relative ease. Chicken (whom Ox had killed with relative ease) gave Boar's corpse a Sky Burial, leaving no trace of flesh behind. Ox was not aware of this, as it hadn't come up in their short conversation, nor had he seen it with his own eyes. But Ox was the Natural-Born Slayer after all and had been able to correctly surmise the zombies' weakness from something else he had seen not long before.

What he had seen was the charred remains that had once been Horse (whom Ox hadn't been able to kill with relative ease). The giant warrior had been steamed alive in the locked vault—though the direct cause of death had been a lack of oxygen—but either way, his dead body was, in fact, dead.

Just as Tiger had gone to investigate the fire, so had Ox. When he arrived at the bank, he found Horse dead with the giant's jewel already freed from his stomach. At the time, Ox didn't think much of it—the master swordsman had not been moved by any petty desire to kill his escaped enemy—but now, he saw as plain as a burning flame that the necromanticist's minion had killed Horse. And yet Horse had not joined the other walking dead. There must have been a logical explanation. By following that line of logic, Ox had been able to single-handedly land upon a method to kill the undead corpses for good.

Ox stood, his momentary display of weakness now over. He wasn't healed by any measure, but the battle was not yet finished, and this was no time to rest.

He glanced at Tiger, whose flames had died out, and explained, "To put it simply, I killed him again with fire. It's the cells in his body. If you cook them, they'll go through necrosis, and he won't be able to move anymore."

At first, Ox's unexplained gambit had thrown her into confusion, but even as drunk as she was, she was still an experienced warrior and had clued in to the general idea. She hadn't reached the same logical conclusions—that the necromanticist's legion was vulnerable to fire, or anything about cellular necrosis—but considering her throat was being crushed, such a realization couldn't be expected of anyone. She did, however, understand that Ox was trying to burn the corpse's arms. Even as she rolled on the asphalt to extinguish her flames, and even as the reanimated arm continued crushing her throat, she held the thing tightly against her chest—and she burned the arm to a final death.

As the flames died down, the tenacious arm finally lost its grip and went slack.

But now she howled, "You bastard!" Even though she owed Ox her life, he had set her on fire without so much as a word, and she wasn't about to meekly bow her head and give him her thanks.

"I'm going to kill you! You think I'm going to treat you like some kid playing with fire? You're dead!" She hurled another growl at him.

"If you're feeling that lively," Ox said to the raging Tiger, "then you must still be up for our fight. None of your burns look to be too bad either."

As she didn't offer her gratitude, he didn't offer an apology. Perhaps he thought he had done nothing wrong—he had taken extreme but appropriate measures and only after properly securing her cooperation. Whatever the case, he decided that this conversation was over. He turned his gaze from Tiger and gently picked up the saber he had so roughly mistreated, even if the emergent situation had required it.

Then he moved his attention to unfinished matters.

Snake's headless, armless corpse had finally managed to stand.

"Well," Ox said, "this is more of a predicament than I'd expected." Despite having just lived through a near-death crisis,

Ox remained as gloomy as always—but he had good reason to, as he was without the means to deal with the walking torso. He knew what he needed to do—burn the abomination like he'd burned its arms—but he had no more fuel for a fire. In killing the arms, Ox had exhausted Tiger's fuel.

Even worse, it would require a much larger blaze to burn an entire body—or an almost entire body, in Snake's case. If a gas station had been nearby, that might have solved their problem, but Ox and Tiger weren't so lucky. An electric-car charging station stood pointlessly within sight. Ox dismissed it, since shocking a corpse might only make it more active.

That left Ox with only his saber—but any foolhardy slicing-and-dicing would only result in a repeat of the macabre slapstick routine. If Ox cut off the corpse's legs, they could crawl their way to him and have another go at crushing him, and the same could be said of the corpse's innards. Slicing apart the corpse was worse than ineffective, it was countereffective.

As an aside, it should be noted that not every necromanticist operated under these same rules. The walking dead existed in many forms, and some zombies could be stopped by simply crushing their heads. Snake's corpse owed its extreme tenacity to both Rabbit's talents as a necromanticist, which transcended typical limits, and to Snake's superiority as a warrior.

Earth's Guidance—Snake's sonar-like ability to grasp his surroundings via vibrations in the earth—gave his various scattered, severed parts the ability to keep on fighting. If he hadn't been killed before the Zodiac War began and had been allowed to participate in the battle as was his right, he might have been able to fight his way into a spot among the favored winners. Earth's Guidance, if used properly, could have given him the understanding of everything that happened in the abandoned city, whether outside, inside, or underground. Such an awareness would have provided him an incredible advantage. Perhaps Rabbit had understood this and decided to eliminate and convert this formidable rival to his side at an early—too early—moment.

With a growl, Tiger—who now reeked more of char than booze—stood and joined Ox in facing the corpse. Rather, she didn't stand, but got on all fours. She said, "After this, you and I are gonna talk."

"And I'll listen. Now, can I count on you to work with me until we defeat this thing?"

Tiger responded with another growl—whether that meant yes or no was anyone's guess. Whatever the case, she didn't turn her claws on Ox at that moment. But she also understood that her nails wouldn't be effective against the younger twin's corpse—like Ox's saber, they would only make the situation worse. Anything she scratched or tore from the zombie would only add to its number.

Never in its entire history had the Zodiac War seen such a ridiculous scenario as two top-favored combatants facing an already dead enemy, yet being entirely unable to act.

Except they can act, Dragon thought as he watched the battle from far above. *My brother is the one who can't. Without his head or his arms, he can't take on those two fighters at once. Besides, this isn't even the kind of stand-off where the first to move will lose. My unfortunate little brother's primary mission is to chase after that kid. If Ox and Tiger realized that and simply turned their backs and fled, the battle would be over just like that. I'd love to see that prodigy, Ox, turn tail for once in his life. On the other hand, this might be my time to act...*

Dragon had been waiting above the skies for the right moment, and he was prepared to wait as long as it took, but this seemed like it might be his best chance. What better opportunity would there be to make a surprise attack on the mighty Ox and Tiger than when both were injured? Dragon was willing to wait longer, but he'd never have a better chance to put himself on the board.

And here I'd thought our days as a team were over, little bro. Not even I saw this coming—I guess we brothers have a bond stronger than death. Anyway, I'm your big brother—it's my job to be the superhero coming to your rescue.

Now, which should he kill with that first surprise strike? For a moment, Dragon considered Tiger—after being set on fire, she seemed like she would have the fewest remaining hit-points and made for the easier target—but in the end, Dragon's decision was easy. Remove the more dangerous adversary first: Ox.

I'm counting on you, little bro. Keep them distracted. I'll hold a memorial service for you.

At the last moment before his rapid descent, he declared himself with determination in his voice.

"I am Tatsumi the Elder, the Fighter of the Dragon. I kill for the money."

"I am Tatsumi the Younger, the Fighter of the Snake. I kill for the money."

Dragon thought he heard his brother's voice in unison with his. It must have been an illusion, a trick of his ears—but then something that was not at all an illusion fell into his hands with a *plop!*

What could possibly have fallen into his hands from above, when he was already above the birds, and the clouds, and the very skies themselves?

His brother's head.

Some time had passed since the head was severed, and it hadn't been particularly well preserved, but there was no mistaking his twin's face. This was no illusion—it was really him. The surprise left Dragon dumbstruck, and he nearly fumbled the severed head, but his mind immediately went to work, attempting to find a logical explanation.

Is this something like a rain of frogs falling from the skies? No, I'm higher than the clouds, and I've never heard of a rain of severed heads. So then the head didn't fall from somewhere above me—it was thrown from somewhere below! Someone launched it to heights even higher than my own, and I caught it on the way down.

But who had thrown his brother's head so high and for what purpose? The who was without question—Rabbit, who held control over Snake's corpse. With that in mind, the second answer became just as clear—to search for Dragon, who was nowhere to be found on the ground.

Dragon had seen Rabbit hang his brother's head from a tree as a makeshift surveillance camera. Now the necromanticist was using it like a drone—one that went higher than the Eye of the Cormorant and even Heavens' Holding.

What—what is Rabbit trying to accomplish?

The necromanticist couldn't have guessed that Dragon was hiding above the skies, but regardless, the elder twin had been found. Snake's eyes—once familiar, but now clouded and unrecognizable—locked onto Dragon's face and relayed the image to his supposed friend down below.

Damn! I became so absorbed in my brother's battle that I lost track of what the others were doing. But there's no need to panic. Remain calm. Rabbit knows where I am now, but what can he do about it? Not even Ox, the Natural-Born Slayer, could attack me up here!

As long as Dragon remained where he was, he would be safe. That would mean giving up his chance to help his little brother on the ground below, but that was then, and this was now. More important than killing Ox and Tiger was ensuring his own safety—

"Ow!"

A jolt of pain shot through Dragon's upper arm. He'd been careless. The object in his hands might have been a severed head—his younger twin's severed head at that—but it was still the necromanticist's minion. As had Snake's severed arms, the severed head remained a member of the walking dead—or at least, the moving dead. The decapitated head bit down with all the force and tenacity of its former namesake.

Of all the times for our first brothers' quarrel!

Dragon attempted to pry his brother's head from his arm. He was lucky Snake hadn't gone for his neck. This way, at worst, he'd only lose his arm.

All of Dragon's attention went to dealing with the immediate danger, but his brother's bite was more effective than he thought it could be. Snake always had given everything his all.

This wasn't the kind of zombification that spread by bite— that wasn't the issue. But the pain took Dragon's focus, if only for one moment, from where it should have remained: on the ground below. One moment was all it took.

That one moment invited his death.

The next moment, a rabbit had leaped in front of him—a rabbit wielding two massive, long-bladed, hatchetlike weapons.

"How—?" Dragon gasped.

Rabbit said, "Haven't you heard the legend of the bunny who jumped all the way to the moon?

"I am Usagi, the Fighter of the Rabbit. I kill with distinction."

In one smooth horizontal motion, Rabbit's twin blades cleaved the elder brother's torso in two.

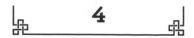

4

The brothers' bond was stronger than death. This was more true now than ever as they reunited under Rabbit's banner, and the elder twin's corpse, much like a superhero, hurtled gallantly toward his little brother's rescue.

RABBIT VS. ~~DRAGON~~

END OF THE 8ᵀᴴ BATTLE

THE NINTH BATTLE

"He who chases after two rabbits will catch neither."

**USAGI,
THE FIGHTER
OF THE RABBIT**

"I wish for friends."

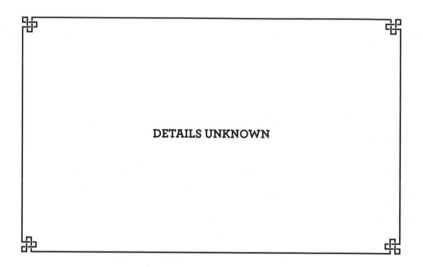

DETAILS UNKNOWN

1

O f course, bunnies couldn't jump to the moon. That amount of jumping power didn't exist in the realm of biology, and Usagi, necromanticist and Fighter of the Rabbit, did not possess that exceptionally superior of a physique. The realm above the skies should have belonged solely and incontestably to the elder Tatsumi brother, the Fighter of the Dragon. Rabbit's incursion had been a feat beyond miracle. How then, had the necromanticist soared to such heights?

He had the help of a dear and trusted friend—Sharyū, the Fighter of the Monkey.

Or to be more precise, he had the help of her corpse. Alive, Monkey would almost certainly never have helped him in that way. Alive, she had been a pacifist beyond compare, and she had never used her powers for such a purpose—nor had she ever even considered it. Now that her undead corpse existed only to serve her precious ally, all her restraints had lifted. The hero was once said to be capable of putting an end to any war on earth—perhaps even beyond—were she to decide to finish it by force rather than seek a peaceful resolution. Now, freed from any moral boundaries or physical limiters, she would do anything for her so-called friend.

Her first duty was to hurtle Snake's head as hard as she could into the skies above the abandoned city. Throwing any object straight up was not such an easy task for most people, but it was for her—most feats that would have been difficult for others came easily to her. Rabbit's only worry had been that she might throw Snake's head into orbit or beyond, but even that outcome wouldn't have been ruinous. From the moment Rabbit had gained the allegiance of Monkey's corpse, he secured a decisive advantage in the battle. A small mistake here or there wouldn't prove his downfall.

The dead hero proved herself still capable of heroic feats, and Snake's head traced an almost perfectly vertical path and narrowly avoided breaking free from Earth's pull. The purpose of the throw was, as Dragon had surmised in his final moments, to provide Rabbit a bird's-eye view—much like Chicken's birds had once provided her—so that he could see the state of the battle as it reached the final act.

One reason he chose this course of action was because Snake—cornered by Ox and Tiger—had lost his quarry, Rat. Monkey had thrown Snake's head to hunt down her own former ally, with whom she had shared a hideout. That in itself was ironic, but the greater irony played out when the head's descent led it right into the arms of its brother and genetic match.

Their reunion was entirely a product of happenstance. The chances against it weren't astronomical—at least not literally, as this was a head, not a meteoroid—but it was akin to winning the lottery.

A more romantic view would attribute the chance occurrence to the intangible bond between twins inseparable in their childhood and on the battlefield. Perhaps, even after death, the younger brother wanted them to be together.

On any other trajectory, Snake's head still would have looked down at the arena from above his older twin; Dragon would have been revealed to the necromanticist regardless. But had the severed head not clamped onto its brother's arm, Dragon might have been able to narrowly evade the leaping Rabbit's killing strike.

Rabbit didn't actually leap that high, of course. Monkey had thrown him too. This time, she aimed for that exact place.

The toss was almost out of a cheerleading routine, except without the cheer. While she had been living, the ever-serene pacifist would never have thrown the severed human head or the man with a better physique than her own, yet now she did both without hesitation—even with the understanding that Rabbit wouldn't hesitate to kill Dragon. Now that she was dead, it wasn't a matter of what she understood or didn't understand. Her place was but to unfeelingly carry out Rabbit's commands. If Rabbit had asked her to throw him all the way to the moon, she might have dutifully done so.

When gravity pulled Rabbit back to ground, her role was to catch him. As for Dragon—who had been split in two by Rabbit's crude twin blades, *Sangatsu-usagi* and *Shiro-usagi,* or March Hare and White Rabbit—his two halves retained the power of flight, even in death, and as such required no catching. Besides, Rabbit didn't coddle his new recruits. All of his friends held equal standing, whether rookie or veteran to his team. He didn't play favorites, instead issuing orders equally to all—for the new recruits, this made for a kind of on-the-job training.

Even as he made his rapid descent, Rabbit quickly issued a command to Dragon's separate halves—to make full and free use of their power of flight to go to their brother's aid. Rather than send them away, he could have used them to carry him safely to ground, but the duty of the leader was to believe in his team—and he believed that Monkey would catch him.

As he plummeted downward, fulfilling his leader's duty, he counted on his fingers. "Rat, Ox, Tiger—only three are left."

2

Unaware of Team Rabbit's impending charge, Ox and Tiger continued their standoff with Snake's headless, armless corpse. In truth, the three weren't in a true deadlock—Dragon's read of the situation had been accurate. If Ox and Tiger wanted to flee, they could have. But that option was closed to them by Ox's warrior pride and Tiger's rage at nearly being killed. The moment seemed like it could have stretched on in perpetuity.

Then, as if dropped by a bomber plane in the far-off skies, the upper and lower bodies plunged down and shattered the standoff.

The lower body landed, cracking the pavement, while the upper body hovered roughly one meter off the ground. The pair made for a surrealistic splatter-flick sight. That Dragon had achieved flight, one of mankind's great aspirations, might have once made him the subject of envy, but Ox regarded the dead man's severed upper body, floating forlornly without its lower half, with unbridled contempt. Elevating the sight from splatter-horror to a grotesque and surrealistic farce was the object cradled gently in its arms—a severed head with an identical face. More than anything else, Ox despised the way Rabbit made playthings of the dead.

But unlike Snake, Dragon had been freshly killed, and blood gushed from where he had been cut open. Tiger's Drunken Fist was more fueled by blood than booze, and the sight somewhat sobered her rage. She even growled in anticipation. These were not the habits of a fighter, but those of a drunkard—yet she didn't leap into battle. Realizing that the stalemate had now made a dramatic turn for the worse, she backed away.

When Dragon plummeted from the skies, so too did Ox and Tiger's fortunes plummet. Their two-to-one advantage had become two-to-two.

Rather, it was four-to-two.

They faced four opponents: Snake's headless, armless corpse; Dragon's upper body; Dragon's lower body; and Snake's head, currently in Dragon's arms. Even worse for Ox and Tiger—though they had no way of knowing it—Rabbit had issued Snake a new command. Snake now shared a mission with his brother; the twin scourges of the battlefield were reunited in battle.

The younger twin had been instructed to kill Ox and Tiger. Up until now, Ox and Tiger could have broken free from the fight simply by running away. Now that option was blocked to them.

Rabbit was bringing the war to an end. The necromanticist hadn't pulled Snake off his pursuit because he was saving the sleepy boy for later. Rather, as a result of the severed head's aerial reconnaissance, he had narrowed down the youth's escape route and sent the nearby Monkey to deal with him.

The Twelfth Zodiac War neared its final stages, and only four challengers remained. Rabbit only needed to kill Rat, Ox, and Tiger, and the victory would be his. This called not for restraint but for a swift conclusion. When he considered that all Rat had done so far was scurry about, only Ox and Tiger truly stood between him and victory.

None of this was lost on Ox. Now that the necromanticist had set all his forces to attack, the swordfighter knew the Zodiac War was drawing to a close. He understood that to stall for time only risked the arrival of further reinforcements.

"Tiger," Ox said. "Do you have any bright ideas? Some kind of special ability that can get us out of this? Maybe you can fly or glide along the ground."

"Sorry, all I've got is my Drunken Fist. I don't have anything that can deal with enemies who refuse to die even after I rip them to shreds."

"I see. Well, don't feel bad. I don't have anything either."

Perhaps less than any other warrior of the day, Ox had no special ability—the saber-wielder just killed—and he might have been the least suited to this kind of aberrant adversary. But even if Rabbit weren't a necromanticist, a meeting between him and Ox could only conclude with one of their deaths—they possessed two distinct forms of genius that the swordfighter could never reconcile.

"I'm not much for trickery," Ox said, "and it's been a while since I've had to devise some strategy—but there's a time for everything. I want you to take a look at that floating half. Do you recognize that thing strapped to its back?"

Confusion in her voice, Tiger said, "Isn't it a flamethrower like his brother's?"

"If anything, it's the opposite—an icethrower. The tank probably contains liquid hydrogen."

"So? What's liquid hydrogen do?"

"Don't you see? It can—"

But before Ox could finish, the battle started. The opposing side's wordless strategy session had concluded first—more likely due to the brothers' lifelong history of teamwork than to the necromanticist's leadership.

The elder twin threw his younger brother's head like a shot put ball toward Ox. Rather than lodge any complaint at the indignity, Snake's mouth opened wide, ready to sink his teeth into the swordfighter. Even at three centimeters long, a snake will try to swallow a man.

Slicing the head with his saber wasn't an option, and catching it posed an unnecessary risk. He could have dodged the head, but doing so would put it somewhere behind him, and he couldn't predict what would happen next. It was a small object, and if it hid somewhere out of sight, dealing with it would become far more difficult. The head might come at him from the shadows and bring about a repeat of the same crisis from which he'd just escaped. Worst case, the thing could bite him on the neck.

Left with no other choice, Ox kicked the head straight up. It was the appropriate response but also exactly what the twins had wanted him to do. As the head spun upward, its eyes acted as a 360-degree panoramic camera. What Snake's head saw, it transmitted not only to his headless, armless body, but directly to Dragon's two halves as well, with no need for Rabbit to act as interlocutor. With Snake's head in the air, they secured an overwhelmingly advantageous view of the battle.

Certainly, Dragon's upper half could have simply thrown the head into the air, but he also sought to create an opening in Ox's guard. The two deceased twins intended to settle this fight before the head came back down—or rather, Rabbit intended it for them. The necromanticist instinctively sensed that a prolonged fight against the Natural-Born Slayer would not be to his advantage. Just as he was Ox's natural enemy, Ox was his.

"I am Tatsumi the Elder, the Fighter of the Dragon. I kill for the money."

"I am Tatsumi the Younger, the Fighter of the Snake. I kill for the money."

That was what they would have said had they still been alive. Ox and Tiger prepared themselves for the twins' attack—coming from three directions.

"I am Ushii, the Fighter of the Ox. I just kill."

"I am Tora, the Fighter of the Tiger. I kill with drunken power."

Though the two were expert fighters and favored champions, their announcement did not strike the corpses with awe. Nothing could deter the emotionless attack of the undead. When the rush came, it was dizzying, and more varied and three-dimensional than any Ox or Tiger had ever faced.

Not only did Dragon have a bird's-eye view of the battle, he possessed the power of flight. Though only his upper body had been floating from the start, his lower half carried the same ability, and it jumped from the ground; then without its feet touching the ground, it leaped again in the air, like a video game character's double jump.

Not only did its attack come from an impossible direction, the zombie's joints pivoted in unnatural ways. At the same time, Dragon's upper half hurtled at Ox from directly above with a twirling corkscrew punch, and Ox could only defend himself.

Their enemies came not only from above, but from below as well. As dragons attacked from the skies, snakes struck from the ground. In their earlier battle, Snake had come at Tiger with a snake fist stance, but now he attacked the woman like a snake itself, rolling and slithering nimbly across the ground.

Feeling every vibration not just with his feet but his entire body, he unleashed a merciless flurry of kicks upward toward Tiger, even as she was on her hands and knees. Between the view from the head in the sky and the vibrations of the earth, he could read her every movement. Like Ox, Tiger could do nothing but defend herself.

Improvising their tactics, Ox and Tiger stood back to back, eliminating any blind spots. They had to be master fighters to be able to defend themselves from this unprecedented and omni-directional assault—but the Tatsumi brothers transcended mortal limits.

Even had the twins been less capable, circumstances prevented Ox and Tiger from making an effective counterattack. The pair could only defend, without use of saber-edge or claws, because the more they sliced and shredded, the more their enemies would increase in number. They understood that one mistake would mean a repeat of their near-death experience.

By remaining calm and focused, they could hold their defenses. No matter how varied and three-dimensional the assault, the zombies were sluggish. Ox's saber and Tiger's Drunken Fist could handle the task—yet it was only a matter of time before they slipped up.

Another strike against the temporary allies was their relative lack of experience on the defensive; both favored the attack. Ox and Tiger were even less accustomed to a defensive battle than they were to fighting as a team—and defense could only carry them so far. Brawny, stalwart Horse had specialized in defense, but he too fell to Rabbit's forces. Unless Ox and Tiger came up with a plan, nothing would reverse the course of this battle. Even if the situation prevented an attack—*Wait,* Tiger thought, *the situation prevents an attack?*

Then Tiger finally got the idea.

"The liquid hydrogen," she said with a growl.

At last, Tiger had made the connection—she was late, but not too late. She acted immediately. Her target was not Snake's legs with their endless kicks, nor was it Dragon's lower body, which assailed Ox with scissor kicks from unorthodox angles. Her target was Dragon's top half, which doggedly reached for the swordsman's neck. Specifically, she was after Yuki-onna, the icethrower Dragon wore strapped to his back.

She didn't know the weapon's clever name—a reference to the yokai known as Snow Woman—or what its liquid hydrogen could do, but the way Dragon refrained from using the weapon, despite this all-out assault, struck her as peculiar. When she had faced Snake one-on-one, the headless zombie hadn't hesitated to blast her with his liquid fire.

Was the weapon malfunctioning? Tiger dismissed that notion. No, some reason was forcing Dragon to refrain from using the icethrower.

The zombies could only continue their ghoulish, unfeeling attacks because their corpses refused to stay dead—in other words, even though they had already lost their lives, they made a clear effort to avoid any injuries that threatened to end them for good. If Dragon used the icethrower amid the confusion of the melee, he risked hitting his own lower body and Snake's headless, armless corpse. They were willing to risk hitting each other with their punches and kicks, but not with that weapon.

Because freezing them would stop them for good.

On her hands and knees, Tiger roared and leaped toward Dragon's floating upper body, and the two beasts clashed. Just as she had done with his brother's flamethrower, she ripped the tank from Dragon's back. She had to tear through the strap, and her nails left deep scratches in the tank and even accidentally tore off one of the floating corpse's arms, but once she had Yuki-onna and the tank full of liquid hydrogen, that would be of little concern.

This time, she wasn't about to drink the tank's contents— she had a different purpose for the liquid hydrogen.

At that very same moment, Snake's head—the would-be panoramic camera—was nearly upon Ox again, falling down at him from straight above. The swordfighter would now have to defend himself from unfamiliar attacks coming from three different directions at once. If Tiger were clever and dastardly, she could have waited for him to succumb. Had she done that, she could have put an end to not only the brothers Dragon and Snake, but her most formidable adversary in the Zodiac War.

But Tiger was not clever, nor was she dastardly. She raised the cracked canister high and hurled it with all her might. When it hit the ground, the suddenly vaporizing hydrogen exploded into a subzero cloud. Not a sky burial or a crema-tion, the cryonic preservation nevertheless proved itself al-most too effective against the corpses.

Snake and Dragon, in all their parts, were frozen solid into an ice-sculpture menagerie. No follow-up would be needed. Dragon's upper and lower halves lost their power of flight and came crashing down and then shattered against the ground, as did the newly severed arm. Snake's headless, armless corpse, already on the ground, took a direct hit from his also plummeting head, and both shattered. Not only their bones, but their skin and flesh and everything were reduced to shaved ice-sized slivers. The twins' bodies scattered and comingled so that there was no telling which brother was which. They were countless, and they were one.

The brothers would never be separated again.

Having broken free from the tangle just in the nick of time, Ox said, "I'm glad you picked up on my idea." Then, without bitterness, he added, "Although you could have said something first."

Tiger's tricky maneuver, which took her weaving through their enemies, made for flashy display, but Ox deserved equal regard for keeping them occupied until the last possible moment. If he had broken away even a moment earlier, the severed head would have instantly transmitted its panoramic view to the others, and at the very least, Snake's headless, armless corpse would likely have escaped the deep freeze.

Tiger growled. "You're one to talk. How the hell was I supposed to know what to do when you're so damn vague?"

"Those corpses could still see. I didn't want to spell it out in case they could hear too." Ox sighed. "I'm just not used to having to pull any tricks like that. I should stick with what I know. At least it all worked out this time."

Provoking him, Tiger said, "What would have worked out for me was you being flash-frozen along with those freaks."

Returning the provocation, Ox said, "Is that so? I haven't forgotten my promise to challenge you to a duel." When Tiger didn't say anything back, he added, "But I think we'll be extending our temporary partnership for just a little while longer. You've noticed, haven't you?"

"Of course I have. That old man Sheep was much better at hiding than this one." Then she roared, "Hey! Come on out, you bastard!"

Then, as a wild hare might emerge from its burrow, Rabbit appeared from behind a sculpture in front of a nearby building, not out of obedience but by his own volition—or maybe he was obeying. He remained impossible to read.

Despite a pair of minions being reduced to frozen smithereens, Rabbit appeared unafraid. He stepped toward Ox and Tiger as his usual composed self, armed with an inexhaustible will to kill, along with those two giant blades—Shiro-usagi and Sangatsu-usagi—the cursed weapons with which he had created so many corpses. Rather, the curse belonged to him, not his weapons.

To Rabbit, Ox said, "I trust you won't complain about facing the two of us—after all, you've been fighting on a team yourself."

Whether or not Rabbit was listening, the necromanticist ignored the comment and announced himself.

"I am Usagi, the Fighter of the Rabbit. I kill with distinction."

His demeanor was perplexing given the circumstances— he had come to join his minions in their fight but arrived only moments too late, only to find himself thrust into an unexpected crisis. Having sent Monkey after Rat, he now faced Ox and Tiger alone. When confronted with this hopeless battle, he showed no signs of despair—but how could one lose hope when he'd gone his whole life without having it?

Such a fighter was beyond Ox's understanding, and though Tiger herself was a renegade, she was made of different stuff. All the more reason to fight.

Though nations would be won or lost based on its outcome, the Zodiac War was also a battle for survival.

"I am Ushii, the Fighter of the Ox. I just kill."

"I am Tora, the Fighter of the Tiger. I kill with drunken power."

For the second time in the same day, Ox and Tiger announced themselves together.

Though Rabbit was a living man, he—like his corpse allies—remained unperturbed by the display of conviction from two expert warriors. Wielding the twin blades, he attacked as if this were routine.

But to fighters like Ox and Tiger, his movements were clumsy; they could have handled his attack with their eyes closed. Compared to the Tatsumi brothers, he might as well have been a bunny bounding in for a snuggle—but Ox and Tiger were not about to go easy on him. They met his attack with blade and Drunken Fist.

Two swift saber slashes struck Rabbit; then after the briefest delay, so did two swipes of ten claws. Rabbit's body fell into eight pieces.

Rabbit failed to offer an interesting fight, but he was a necromanticist, after all, who employed corpses to do his fighting—and he went with no prolonged death scene either; no villain's dying scream, no final words. That was it. The vast gap in ability and skill left Rabbit no time to feel surprise. In the face of Tiger and Ox—who was fighting ability distilled into human form—Rabbit stood not a chance on his own.

Thus died the mysterious man who had thrown the Twelfth Zodiac War into a greater turmoil than any combatant had done in the history of the event.

Not missing a beat, Ox said to Tiger, "Well then," seemingly feeling no deep emotion at the killing of this formidable adversary; no matter who the enemy, no matter what curse they bore, once dead they were of no further concern. "Would you rather take a short break first, Fighter of the Tiger?"

Licking the necromanticist's blood from her nails, Tiger said, "Don't make me laugh, Fighter of the Ox," as if Rabbit had never mattered to her at all. "This blood has me nice and drunk. Now, put up a good fight, will you? I want to have some fun."

"All right. Then our alliance is now over," Ox said, removing a glove and throwing it at Tiger. "It's a duel."

3

Rabbit had been killed. He had been sliced into pieces—that much was true.

But before he was sliced into pieces, he had bitten his own tongue off and instantly choked on it. That he had made no dying scream and given no final words was a matter of course.

Rabbit had killed himself, and the wounds left by the nimble saber slashes and the savage claw swipes came after his suicide.

One might ask, *He's dead—so what the heck does it matter how he died?*

In normal cases, that would be true. But Rabbit wasn't normal—he was a necromanticist who wielded control over those he killed.

What would happen when a man like that killed himself?

Ox and Tiger were about to find out.

OX AND TIGER VS. ~~RABBIT~~
END OF THE 9TH BATTLE

THE TENTH BATTLE

"When a tiger dies, it leaves its hide behind."

**TORA,
THE FIGHTER
OF THE TIGER**

"I wish for rightness."

REAL NAME: **Kanae AIRA**

BORN: **January 1**

HEIGHT: **154 cm**

WEIGHT: **42 kg**

Kanae claims to use the Drunken Fist technique, but the true style only imitates drunken movements—the consumption of alcohol is not actually required. It would be more accurate to say that she took up Drunken Fist as an excuse to drink. In truth, she possesses extensive knowledge of martial arts beyond her favored method. The Aira are a military clan focused on hand-to-hand combat, and Kanae is quite a remarkable warrior, even among them.

One downside to the Drunken Fist style is that its users are often told they don't look strong, but Kanae in turn believes that only the truly weak need to make a show of strength. Naturally, over time, she became less and less of a visible threat. One could go so far as to say that making a show of weakness was her defining feature. She was incredibly, exceptionally good at it, even if it wasn't a conscious act.

Her fingernails were her only weapon, and being killed by her was a terribly painful way to die. If a survey among her peers asked whom they would least like to face on the battlefield, she would be ranked higher than her relatively infrequent deployments would otherwise suggest.

She likes to keep elaborate decorations on her nails, but before she goes into battle, she always removes her polish. She just wouldn't feel right killing her enemies with decorated nails.

On her days off, she likes to go shopping with her lady friends, and they inevitably end up going out for drinks.

1

As perplexing as the White Rabbit and as bewildering as the March Hare, Usagi, the Fighter of the Rabbit, ended his remarkably spirited performance as if snatching defeat from the jaws of victory—but his loss was not caused by a failure to take the battle seriously. The necromanticist's thoughts were impenetrable to others, and he was a thoroughly odd man, but if nothing else, he approached the Zodiac War in total earnest.

Though his enemies would have preferred a less enthusiastic adversary, he hadn't blatantly cheated as did Sheep, and he hadn't actively avoided the fighting as had Rat and Dragon. Viewed objectively, none had matched Rabbit's diligence in pursuit of the war.

A man like that had most definitely not revealed himself to Ox and Tiger out of simple incaution.

Most observers would likely consider his death the result of a foolish mistake. Though Rabbit had correctly concluded that his minions Dragon and Snake required reinforcements, he could have pursued Rat—the other remaining, and less threatening, enemy—and sent his strongest asset, Monkey, to kill Ox and Tiger instead. Surely that would have been the better strategy—despite his tremendously advantageous ability to befriend those he killed, the necromanticist's actual talent for combat was decidedly lacking.

In hindsight, Monkey would also have arrived too late to prevent the twins being frozen, but the overwhelmingly powerful fighter would have forced Ox and Tiger into their toughest battle yet.

That said, sending Monkey after Ox and Tiger was only the right choice if winning the Zodiac War was Rabbit's sole concern. If you looked at it from Rabbit's perspective—that of a necromanticist who took a medium-term rather than a short-term view—his goals should become clear. Granted, putting one's self in the mind of that mad hare might be a stretch for an upstanding citizen, but the key point is this: winning the Zodiac War wasn't going to end the necromanticist's battles.

No matter how strange or how inscrutable the man was, Rabbit was a warrior. Once he won this war, the next would be waiting. When he won that war, then would come another. As long as he kept on winning, he would have to keep on fighting; such was a warrior's fate.

His necromanticist's instinct was to secure the undead allies that might give him a needed advantage in the next fight. There was no telling how much easier his next battle would be with the Natural-Born Slayer on his side—or even Tiger of the Drunken Fist. Their corpses would eventually rot, but they would remain valuable for some time.

Rabbit viewed fighting—or in other words, making corpses—as his only way of making friends. He sent himself to join the fight against Ox and Tiger not because he believed his help was needed—he had come with his dual blades to finish them off. Though he trusted his allies, this was something he felt he needed to do himself. Were they anyone else besides Ox and Tiger, he would have left them to the twins.

When his corpses killed for him, they could go too far— an inevitable consequence of the zombies' lack of any restraint or inhibition. When Snake roasted Horse to death, Rabbit lost his chance to befriend the stalwart warrior—and harness Stirrup, Horse's defensive ability. The necromanticist had ultimately found a use for the birds shredded and killed by Boar's machine guns, but if he left Ox and Tiger to his undead and unfettered helpers, he risked his new friends becoming damaged beyond usefulness. And so, he decided he would be the one to finish them off.

With the Zodiac War's end in sight, he turned his attention to what would happen after. Such presumptive thinking came with its advantages and drawbacks, but as a warrior he had to think that way—as such, his decision to join the fight wasn't an outright mistake. If any flaw existed in his reasoning, it was the assumption that Ox and Tiger couldn't possibly defeat the Tatsumi brothers with such haste and relative lack of injury.

He didn't base this assumption on the brothers' lifelong history as a team or their close connection as twins— the necromanticist simply hadn't imagined that the free-willed pair of Ox and Tiger could prevail over the undead who had no free will. With no minds of their own, Snake and Dragon would never betray each other, but Ox and Tiger should have—at least at some point—been at odds. He couldn't have conceived his allies would be so ignominiously routed.

When faced with this impossible truth—that living people too could forge bonds of trust, Rabbit knew he had lost—and so, he chose death.

But he didn't choose death out of despair.

For the necromanticist, the Zodiac War was not yet over.

2

Seeing Tora, the Fighter of the Tiger, as she was now, it might be hard to believe, but at the time she first went into combat she was a deeply contemplative and serious woman—too much so at times. Raised in a military clan and tutored on their training grounds, she was taught that fighting, with its barbarism and violence, was her path.

When she ventured onto the real battlefields, she thought and felt in too much earnest. Unable to switch off her mind, she ruminated over each of her commanders' orders. She found herself thinking, *Why do people have to fight each other?* and *How much worth is in a life?* It only progressed from there. As she danced through blades and bullets, she tormented herself with thoughts like *Do humans deserve to live?* and *Wouldn't the world be better off if we went extinct?*

She was too pure for that way of life—pristine even. She lacked that tainted quality that enabled others to shunt away or repress feelings of guilt and awareness of surrounding corruption. As she continued killing her enemies, her actions stayed with her, and her misgivings grew heavier, eventually affecting her in her daily life.

She began to see the world as filled with hypocrisy and contradiction. What she had once seen as just and right was now mere façade; what she had once seen as harmful evil was what propped up the system from within.

She had believed she fought to bring about peace but realized the insignificance of her accomplishments as an individual: that in saving someone, she hurt someone else. When she thought she'd saved a country, the new government collapsed under its own illegitimacy. The more she fought, the more the wars increased in scale. Eventually, she realized that she was being sent into wars for the purpose of further intensifying the conflicts.

It was also true that without those battlefields, some people would have no reason to live. Fighting brought happiness to many people, and an equal measure could find happiness in only that way.

Her belief that she was doing the right thing seemed nothing more than a cliché now. To consider herself a good person would have been about as meaningful as the summary on the back cover of a children's picture book.

Her life's path was nothing more than a paved road.

Except there wasn't even a road at all.

She felt as if she was walking on a muddy expanse, a bog sloshing stickily under every footstep, threatening to twist her ankles—and just as no fish would live in waters that were completely pure, no road could be built upon unstable earth.

And yet everyone else constantly extolled their ideals; rather than admit the world was corrupt, they spouted pretenses of morals and the ability to tell right from wrong. When she thought about the ridiculousness of all the artifice, Tiger felt like she could puke.

To hold fast to her path would be to face constant pressure coming from all sides to turn that path astray. As much as she tried to walk straight, as straightforward as she tried to live, the world would never permit her to continue. Wherever she went, the road ahead of her was closed for construction.

In the end, Tiger left her path.

Before anyone else changed her course, she left it of her own free will—by turning to alcohol.

When she was drunk, she didn't have to think. Nothing troubled her anymore. The contradictions of the world that had weighed upon her never entered her swaying vision. If her footsteps were caught in a mire, she could simply crawl instead. On her hands and knees, she didn't feel so nauseous.

For better or worse, Tiger didn't become a pacifist like Monkey. It wasn't because she was too weak or a bad person—she was simply too innocent for it. She didn't have Monkey's good kind of stubbornness or Chicken's bad kind either.

Ironically, the more Tiger pickled herself in alcohol, the better a warrior she became. It was as if her talents had been awakened—though despite her claims, she didn't become stronger the more she drank. Rather, the alcohol saturated her mind, erasing all the troubles that had settled inside her and leaving no room for other unnecessary thoughts. Those thoughts and troubles—or, by another name, her sense of ethics and morals—had been cast aside. Whenever she began to remember them, she drank whatever she could find, no matter what kind or what proof.

She'd often been told her heavy drinking was physically harmful, but she preferred drinks that were bad for her body over thoughts that were bad for her mind. If the world in which she believed was rotten, then she could rot a little too.

She stopped caring what became of her. She truly thought she'd be better off if her very blood fermented into alcohol. The earnest and hearty girl had grown into a cynical and unhealthy adult—or, if that's too redundant, she became an adult. In a way, that was what growing up was.

Tiger thought she was just going through a slump, like could happen to anyone. Anyone could have a setback and could become discouraged. She began only to go into battle when she felt like it, and her fighting grew increasingly perfunctory. Despite this, she still got results, and her reputation increased rather than plummeted. This approval was another of life's contradictions that continued to hound her.

She received more praise now that she wasn't trying than she had when she took everything seriously. That thought drove her to drink even more. For what had been all her effort? Where had her diligence gotten her? For what had she been striving?

At some point, Tiger started getting drunk on blood. Blood and alcohol were the only things that could make her forget everything else. She had once been a superior student, but now she felt her intellect slowly but steadily wane. No matter how much she lost, it didn't hinder her on the battlefield.

She lost her ability to strategize and started fighting haphazardly. It didn't hinder her. She stopped being able to remember the names of her allies, so she started fighting alone. It didn't hinder her. She lost the ability to read expressions, so she quit looking at her enemies' faces. It didn't hinder her. She stopped being able to tell the difference between who was important and who wasn't, so she started treating everyone as though they were unimportant. It didn't hinder her. She couldn't read maps anymore. It didn't hinder her. She stopped being able to read kanji that had more than six brush strokes. It didn't hinder her. She could still do multiplication, but not division. It didn't hinder her. She had long since become unaware of what day it was, but now had to struggle to remember her own birthday. It didn't hinder her. She could no longer walk in a straight line. It didn't hinder her. She couldn't even tell if she was still alive or if she was dead. It didn't hinder her. None of it did.

Then, one such unhindered day, Tiger met a lone master.

In one exceptionally dire battle, she met a warrior. Rather, she was saved by one. Letting the alcohol do the thinking as always, she had made a reckless charge into what she knew was a trap. She had just wanted to get the fighting over with.

Then a dashing swordsman appeared, and with his saber he dispatched the enemy group in the blink of an eye. His was nice, clean swordsmanship, of the sort she once had admired and aspired to attain. He wielded the blade with such precision that to call the display beautiful wouldn't be doing it justice. In his arm, the saber moved without hesitation, as if he held the conviction that he was doing the right thing in the right way.

He engaged the seemingly limitless enemy in the correct order, taking the shortest appropriate route in the most effective and efficient way. The sight was a bucket of ice water poured over her to wash away her drunken stupor. She couldn't remember how many years had passed since the last time she had been herself and sober. His transcendent swordsmanship cut her to her heart, and she froze, not moving a muscle.

"Are you hurt, young miss? Did they force you to drink? That's dreadful. People like that bring disgrace to all fighters. Don't worry; you're all right now. I'm not going to harm you. I'll take you someplace safe."

Tiger thought, *Young miss? Me?* It was an easy mistake, as she did look rather childish   the regression of her mental age had reached into her appearance. Either way, the warrior seemed to think he had rescued a civilian—and he might not have been wrong at that. Tiger had long since stopped considering herself a warrior. This phase of her life was, at its essence, a cry for help and for someone to save her.

When she spoke, it wasn't to firmly insist she was a warrior, or that she was no "young miss," or that she hadn't needed any rescuing. Instead, falteringly, fearfully, meekly, and with her words all tangled up, she asked how he could do everything so right—how she could do what was right—and do so without hesitation, doubt, or mistake.

He gave her a puzzled look. She blushed, embarrassed by her question, although whether it was noticeable or not was unclear; she remained, in effect, still drunk. No matter how much her thoughts had sobered, her cheeks had been flushed from the start.

"Hmm," he said. Apparently, the puzzled look was not directed toward her but toward the question itself. "I've never thought about it before. Tell me, young miss, do you want to do the right thing?"

She responded with a demure nod. She couldn't remember the last time she'd done that. Young miss indeed.

He said, "Well, let me think about it. Sometimes it can be good to put one's principles of conduct into words."

He sheathed his saber, and his expression turned thoughtful. Then, moments later, he nodded, seemingly having found his answer—and so quickly, after she had struggled with it for so long.

"First," he said, "you decide to do the right thing." He put his hand on the hilt of his saber. "Then you do it." He drew his sword in a swift, smooth motion, and said, "That is all."

Decide to do the right thing. Then do it.

Her hopes fell—right off a cliff. The philosophy was so esoteric he might as well have not said anything. Maybe he'd tried to simplify it because he thought he was speaking to a child, but if that was the case, he overdid it by far.

She found herself saying she couldn't do that, and that was why she hurt.

It was at that moment she realized she still hurt—that she hadn't forgotten her anguish or washed it away with booze. It had been with her the whole time.

The swordsman said, "Don't you see? The point is that you can't do the right thing unless you first decide to do the right thing. One way or the other, people err. Circumstances carry them into misdeed. Without any reason, without any thought, without any intention, they find themselves having been turned astray, onto the wrong path. The opposite never happens. No one says, 'Without realizing it, I found myself doing the right thing,' or 'At some point I must have started doing good deeds,' or 'I inadvertently did something right.' Without intent, there is no being right. Proper conduct requires proper intent. Without first deciding to do the right thing, you can't do it. If you say you hurt because you can't do the right thing, that's because you haven't decided that's what you want to do."

He'd done his best to simplify it for her, but he didn't pull any punches. Ultimately, his advice remained too abstract for a mere mortal, but his words were just what her tumultuous heart thirsted for, and they stung her core like a disinfecting splash of alcohol in a wound.

The man continued. "There are many reasons not to do the right thing, plenty of causes for indecision and fear. People can blame it on others or on society at large—or even on the times or on fate. But what people who don't do the right thing must understand is that it's not because they can't, but because they don't. You certainly don't have to force yourself to behave the right way, but never allow yourself to forget that the choice was yours to make. Everyone who does right follows the steps: decide, then act. To remain on the first step while fretting over the second is the height of folly."

The master seemed to consider the lesson concluded, but Tiger still didn't fully comprehend it. They were both warriors, but the gap between them was like that between an adult and a child. Despite not understanding, she wanted to. She wanted to become someone who could understand.

Then, despite her being uninjured, he carried her on his back to a nearby town—as if she really was a child—and she didn't object.

When they arrived, he said, "Be careful from now on." Now that he had taken her to safety, he seemed about to return straight to the battle.

Tiger still wanted to talk to him and even faked feeling unwell to try to get him to stay.

"I can't do that," he said flatly. "I have other girls like you to rescue. It's my job. Now, try not to go near a war zone again. I'll pray that you'll never meet another killer—another slayer—like me."

He was right in everything. He walked the right path in the right way. He looked at the contradictions of war with clear eyes, and he battled them head-on.

She felt painfully aware that to him she was just one person among a great many others. She and he were supposedly both warriors, but they weren't the same. She wondered if only people such as he truly had the right to be called warriors—but the thought didn't upset her. Instead, for the first time, she felt as if she had a purpose. She hadn't felt like this when she followed the path she had been taught or when she had decided to stray from it.

The next time I meet that man, she thought, *I want to be someone he can acknowledge as a warrior.*

He told her he would pray that they would never meet again, but he could pray whatever he wanted.

First decide, then do.

She would likely never understand what was right or what purpose fighting held, but at that moment, she decided to start living again. She decided to reexamine the thoughts she had excised from her mind. On that day, she had found someone to inspire her—someone who had built a mighty wall that closed off her previously unhindered life.

3

Tiger didn't have to search long before learning that the master who had given her the incomprehensible advice was also the warrior said by some to be incomprehensibly strong—the Fighter of the Ox—and that his name was Ushii. But the world was large and its battlefields countless. She had been hasty to assume she would encounter him again and was beginning to give up on the idea of ever meeting the master swordsman, when the Zodiac War came.

She went to her family, with whom she had severed nearly all ties, and got on her hands and knees—genuflecting, not crawling—and bowed her head all the way to the floor as she begged them to have her chosen as a competitor. With the next Zodiac War not due for another twelve years, she viewed this as her last chance.

Then, when she saw him, looking as if he hadn't aged a day, on the observation deck at the battle's start, she felt so elated she nearly wanted to dance—and she wasn't even drunk.

And that idiot—that ox of a man—he doesn't remember me at all! It's infuriating!

Now he had challenged her to a duel. Without warning, the enraged woman threw herself at him. To launch a surprise attack without naming herself was a breach of propriety that—to quote Ox when he rescued her long ago—would bring disgrace on all fighters. But she had no choice.

She hadn't the time to say anything—not if she was going to shield Ox from Rabbit's twin blades, which flew at Ox from behind.

When she pushed Ox aside, she unavoidably put herself in his previous position—right in the path of Rabbit's blades.

Ahh, damn it, she thought. *Just when I'd finally made it. Just when the master had finally challenged me to a fight. I couldn't get anything to go right in the end.*

To say she had shielded Ox wasn't strictly true—that would imply he couldn't have handled the attack on his own. Rabbit must have used some aspect of his necromanticist's power to make a puppet of himself, and if he were one of those walking dead, his strength and speed would have been lessened. And yet despite her lesser expertise, the woman still intervened—but why?

Because I decided to.

The twin blades, Shiro-usagi and Sangatsu-usagi, plunged into the softness of her stomach.

Rabbit's severed arms had jumped from the ground to attack. Being just arms, they hadn't the best aim and missed vital points. But the wound was deep—so very deep. Pain didn't even begin to describe what she felt. If another attack came, she couldn't have defended herself.

She closed her eyes, preparing herself for the end, when Ox shouted. For the first time, she heard anger and dismay in his voice.

"Tiger!" he yelled, as he threw himself at Rabbit's eight separate pieces, leaping from one to the other if he were the rabbit, striking each one down.

Without concern for future consequences, Ox carved apart Rabbit's corpse. He knew that the more pieces he created, the more enemies he would later have to face, but getting out of this situation—and getting out now—was his only concern.

He'd saved the arms for last, chopping them to little bits, scattering them to the ground along with the long-bladed hatchets they once held. He grabbed Tiger by the nape of her neck and fled from the multitude of Rabbit parts. He pulled her up and onto his back, then ran blindly and as fast as he could.

Here I am being carried by him again, Tiger thought.

"Don't worry, I won't let you die!" he shouted, trying to keep her conscious, his voice uncharacteristically loud. "No one has ever risked their life to save me—I still have to repay my debt."

What a load of crap, Tiger thought. *I'm the one who owes you for saving my life.*

She said, "Let me down."

Ox drew in his breath.

"It's okay," she said, forcing determination into her voice, even if part of her wanted to just let him keep carrying her. "If you keep bouncing me about, it'll only worsen my injuries."

"Then we'd better stop the blood flow first. We've bought enough distance for now—he shouldn't catch up with us so quickly."

Ox did what he was told. He didn't like the idea of stopping—especially when he imagined what was coming after them—but staunching her bleeding was better done now. He held her face up in his arms, then gently laid her on the ground.

Even to one with his skills, stopping a gut wound from bleeding was not going to be easy. Given the wound's placement, a tourniquet wasn't an option. He'd need to find an abandoned hospital and search for medical supplies—but did they have the time?

We don't, Tiger thought. *We just don't.*

"Don't give up," Ox said. "If you die here, then what becomes of our duel?"

You're just saying that because you're too good to have ever been wounded like this. You don't know what it's like. Even if by some miracle you managed to stitch me up in time…I wouldn't be able to fight. We'll never have that duel. And so…

"Listen, O Fighter of the Ox," Tiger said, still on her back. "I don't need that duel anymore. Just… do me a favor."

"A favor?"

"It's more of a plea. I want you to do one thing for me."

The blood felt like it would never stop.

She growled softly.

If I were just some normal girl, I might ask him for a kiss. But that's not who I am.

"Please," she said, "kill me."

Ox looked at her in disbelief.

She continued, "If I die from losing too much blood… that'll mean that Rabbit bastard will have killed me, won't it? And I'll become one of those walking dead, won't I? I don't know much about that necromanticist and all that stuff… but I don't want any of it. I don't want to fight you badly enough to die for it."

Just having you challenge me to a fight made all my battles worthwhile.

"Before that happens, I want you to kill me," she said. "Didn't you tell me earlier that you'd kill me so that I'd never become one of those wretched zombies? So, Natural-Born Slayer, just kill me. Give me a fine death."

Ox looked down at her for a short time, then said. "All right. But we're going to have that duel. You will lose to me. Now, follow the custom—declare yourself."

Can't you see it's hard for me to speak? Here I am on the edge of death, and you're still going to be this strict? Except...no, you're just doing what's right.

It's a better ending than I deserve—a good-for-nothing like me dying in a duel against a master. At some point along the way, I made a mess of my life, but at least it'll have a proper ending.

"One more thing," Ox said, pointing his saber down at Tiger. "Why do you have a grudge against me? We have met before, on some battlefield, haven't we?"

At first, Tiger said nothing, then she pointed her claws at him. "I've got no grudge. We've never met before. I just hate dreary men like you." She growled.

"I am Tora, the Fighter of the Tiger. I kill with drunken power."

"I am Ushii, the Fighter of the Ox. I just kill."

It was over in an instant. The master did the right thing and killed the dying woman.

She was Tora, the Fighter of the Tiger, drunkard and wielder of the Drunken Fist—and in the history of the Zodiac War, she was the first to lose and still get her wish.

OX VS. ~~TIGER~~

END OF THE 10ᵀᴴ BATTLE

THE ELEVENTH BATTLE

"Using another's burdock to prepare a memorial meal."

**USHII,
THE FIGHTER
OF THE OX**

"I wish to be saved."

REAL NAME: **Eiji KASHII**
BORN: **February 2**
HEIGHT: **181 cm**
WEIGHT: **72 kg**
NICKNAME: **The Natural-Born Slayer**

From his first battle at the age of five, Eiji has killed every enemy he faced. From the start, people called him a natural, and his claim over the title became absolute—so much so that to this day, the only time anyone else is discussed as being a natural is in comparison to him.

His use of the saber is as magnificent as it is precise. Despite lacking any other weapons or remarkable abilities, Eiji can turn the tide of any battle. He has earned the reputation of bringing certain victory to whichever camp draws him to their side.

Eiji himself feels no particular allegiance to country or ideology and acquits himself as a common soldier. To him, winning is a foregone conclusion—what he holds far more important is how to end war. As the warrior who brings a swift end to any conflict, he would have liked to talk to Monkey, who kept wars from reigniting.

He calls his saber *Gobōken*—bayonet—and though the weapon isn't anything special—it was a mass-produced item—he treats it with great care and respect.

Eiji is slim but has a rather large appetite. He doesn't know how to cook and chooses to dine out instead. As a warrior, he abstains from alcohol and knows a lot about restaurants where he can eat alone.

1

This was no time to wallow in sentimentality. Besides, mercy killings such as this were a common occurrence on the battlefield—now there had merely been one more. Killing Tiger before she turned into a zombie hadn't significantly changed the situation Ox was in. He needed to remain calm and clearheaded and make his next move.

Ushii, the Fighter of the Ox, knew all this. And yet, for one uncharacteristic moment, the Natural-Born Slayer held his gaze on Tiger's lifeless body. Except he hadn't been himself for more than just this moment—yes, an ally suffering a grave injury was cause for distress, but he had never before lost control like he did when Tiger was stabbed.

He had carved up Rabbit's corpse without regard for the consequences. He fled combat, and he shouted. None of these were familiar experiences to him. Maybe it was because he saw something in her that reminded him of that girl he met on the battlefield.

Maybe Tiger wasn't her after all, Ox thought.

The girl's questions carried the unsophistication and purity of youth. *How do you do everything so right? How can I do what's right?*

Ox still remembered being taken aback when he was confronted by the questions, which he had never asked himself. Mostly that was because no one else would have been so rudely presumptuous as to spring such sweeping questions on the

Natural-Born Slayer—but the encounter was refreshingly un-expected. Practically everything in his life went as expected and according to plan, and he had been starved of anything bearing an element of surprise—and so he met that refreshing question with a serious answer.

"First, decide to do the right thing," he had said. "Then do it."

By giving form to his outlook and saying it aloud, he felt as if he'd had an awakening. If his genius had been lacking in any way, this was the moment it became complete. In truth, after this encounter, his accomplishments became even more remarkable than before.

I had been rude to treat such a strong warrior as if she were a naive, innocent child. Even though I never drink, I should have liked to make an exception and share one with her.

Though he had been shaken, Ox was still the Natural. Tiger's body only captured his eyes and his empathy for one brief moment, and his mournful prayer lasted just one more, then he refocused his attention on the matter at hand. He was not so overcome by sentimentality to consider giving the woman a burial. He was in the middle of a war held only once every twelve years, and another corpse than hers more urgent-ly required being put to rest.

Usagi, Fighter of the Rabbit...even dead, you're still fighting. In a way, death is supposed to be a release for us warriors—but I suppose a necromanticist wouldn't understand. Even so, to make a puppet out of your own corpse is beyond insanity.

But as much as Ox rejected Rabbit's thinking, he under-stood it to a point. He knew what the necromanticist was attempting to do. Rabbit, recognizing his certain defeat, had chosen to take his own life, but not because he figured he was going to die anyway and could at least take the other fighters down with him and spoil the war's outcome. No, it wasn't that at all.

In death, Rabbit sought victory.

Rabbit found a loophole in the Zodiac War's rules—or if not a hole, then part of its intended design. The judge, Duodecuple, had stated that the only condition for winning the Twelfth Zodiac War was to collect all twelve poison jewels swallowed by the combatants. As much as the contest was a battle royale, direct combat was ultimately not required to win—the only need was to collect the jewels. The rule was simple and broad in scope, capable of providing an exceedingly fair match between greatly varied competitors.

But for all that the rules didn't mention killing, the only way to obtain another fighter's jewel was to reach into their stomachs for it, which made killing a logistical inevitability. The only exception came from challengers like Sheep, who didn't swallow their jewels—but that tactic was clearly out of bounds.

The war would conclude with one of two possible results: all eleven fighters aside from the winner were dead, or the battle went on past the time limit, and any fighters still alive at that time would succumb to the poison and die a pitiful death.

Certainly, some fighters might have survived the poison— though Ox was not among them. Dog, whom Ox hadn't encountered, had neutralized the poison inside his body with the intention of outliving its effects. Ox could imagine the slim possibility that Horse—whose skin had been tough enough to repel the Natural-Born Slayer's attacks—might have been resilient enough internally survive the poison, but even had Horse survived—or if any other fighter did in some other way—they wouldn't have been able to collect all twelve jewels and would not have qualified as the winner.

But to examine the situation from the flipside, any fighter who met the conditions of victory would be the winner—even if that fighter were dead.

This interpretation of the rules—as extreme as it was—led Rabbit to take his own life before he could be killed. He had regarded his life with the same unfeeling attitude he had toward the lives of others. As if merely deciding to take a left turn upon seeing that the right turn was blocked, he recognized that he had no chance at winning alive and instead chose to seek victory dead. Before he ended his conscious existence, he imprinted himself with one command—collect the twelve jewels.

Ox thought, *The judge could have prevented this mess merely by saying that death was grounds for disqualification—but the organizers could never have imagined the necromanticist would do this.*

Or perhaps they had, and this was part of the advantage given to Rabbit. From what Ox had seen, he speculated that all twelve fighters held their own unique advantages against the rules.

Except for myself, that is.

For Ox to desire some advantage above and beyond his incredible innate talents was perhaps shameless. It could be said that his opponents hadn't been given advantages but rather handicaps to even the match against Ox.

No, I did have a significant advantage—by meeting Tiger. If we hadn't fought together, and if I didn't have her help, I would be dead.

In any event, Rabbit had in effect lost the Zodiac War, then created for himself a loser's bracket from which he could remain a contender. That being the case, when he stabbed Tiger in the stomach rather than somewhere more vital, he might not have missed his aim—if he was aiming for the jewel she had swallowed.

I can see his logic. If I remove any emotions from consideration, all of Rabbit's actions can be explained. He's not just showy and bizarre for the sake of it—though unusual in his looks and his methods, he's making all the right moves.

But why was the man willing to go this far? The winner of the Zodiac War could make any single wish. But as long as there was life, there was hope—what wish could a person want so badly to be willing to die for it? If he wanted something that badly, shouldn't he have given up on the contest and applied himself to finding some way to survive?

What had Rabbit decided to do, and what was he doing?

Ox's questions lingered, but he cleared them from his mind. *I don't think I'll ever solve this mystery. Even if I tried to find out what he sought by coming here, I'd have nowhere to start looking. If we couldn't reach any mutual understanding while he was alive, we surely can't now that he's dead. In the end, it doesn't matter. All I can do now is give him a proper funeral.*

Giving Rabbit a funeral might have sounded like a kindness, but Ox really meant a cremation. Incinerating the necromanticist's corpse was the only effective option left to Ox now. Theoretically, he could also freeze the zombie, but liquid hydrogen, or something of the kind, would be hard to find in the abandoned city.

Not that finding fuel and a fire starter will be easy. A gas station might still be my best bet. I could also go from car to car and siphon the gasoline, but that would take a while.

This time, he would have to face the corpse alone, and he remained unaccustomed to devising tricky strategies. As he tried to do so, his thoughts were interrupted.

"What—?" he even said.

He had put enough distance between himself and Rabbit that he thought he'd have a little more time before all the little pieces could catch up—and when Rabbit appeared, it wasn't in pieces.

The carved-up chunks of the necromanticist's corpse had reassembled themselves into the shape reminiscent of a man.

However, the form was only human in rough outline. The mass of parts shared a similar silhouette with Rabbit before his death, but in places all over it had been assembled wrong. His left arm was inside out, his right arm swapped with his left leg, his eyes lodged in his stomach, the top of his head protruding from the bottom of his back, his fingernails jutting out from his chest, his tailbone stuffed in his mouth, his heart exposed, and his fingers crawling around—everything had been so thoroughly jumbled, it was harder to find a part situated in the right place, like a plastic model put together by the whims of a builder lacking instructions or a finished picture.

Part hodgepodge and part patchwork, the parts were bound together by blood vessels and muscle fibers—among other binding agents like coagulated blood as glue, stripped-off skin as wrapping, bone fragments as bracing, and ripped-out wisdom teeth as pins. Though their arrangement was haphazard, the pieces were held secure so that they wouldn't fall apart

Rabbit's blades, Shiro-usagi and Sangatsu-usagi, were there too, included like any other body part. The pieced-together corpse was using the weapons like crutches to help him walk. Since his arms—one of which was actually a leg—were in no shape to hold them, the weapons had been fastened in place with a couple lengths of small intestine.

He isn't even a zombie anymore—he's an abomination.

Through his many battles, Ox had seen dead bodies in terrible, grisly states, but this was the first time he had felt the urge to look away.

Here, too, Rabbit's logic was present. Unlike Dragon and Snake, the necromanticist hadn't the power of flight, nor had he experience with slithering and crawling along the ground. After being chopped up into many pieces, he must have reasoned that the fastest way to catch Ox was to reconstruct himself and walk just like was normal—although of course there was nothing normal about the amalgamated corpse's sluggish shamble.

Disturbing as Rabbit's appearance was, it gave Ox hope.

Being nearly strangled to death left me focused on that tactic—I've been assuming the corpse would attack me in pieces. Depending on the former fighter, a zombie might not consider remaining split up to be an effective choice. If that's the case with Rabbit, chopping him up again might work to my advantage.

It might, but it wouldn't get Ox anywhere new. He might be able to buy himself some time, but it would never finish Rabbit off.

I can't afford to waste my time on this man—not that he's leaving me a choice.

Rabbit was an opponent he'd already defeated. The Zodiac War was still ongoing, and the matador wouldn't get anywhere tied up by Rabbit.

No matter how masterful a fighter Ox was, no matter if he always decisively took the most appropriate course of action, he lacked information. He didn't have any special ability like the Eye of the Cormorant that could give him a bird's-eye view of the battle. He couldn't see the current state of the other warriors—or of the war as a whole. He didn't know that only he and one other fighter remained alive.

He knew of six that had died—Tiger, Dragon, Snake, Horse, Chicken, and Boar. From Chicken's extra jewel, he could assume that she had killed one other, and from what Tiger had said when she mentioned Sheep, the old man was likely dead. But whether or not any or all of the other fighters were still alive, Ox didn't have a reason to waste one extra moment on Rabbit.

So then I'll carve him up one more time and search for a gas station while he's putting himself back together again.

The idea of chopping up Rabbit again was unpleasant—taking his saber to the vulgar monstrosity felt akin to desecrating a corpse—but he saw no other effective option. Though Rabbit's humanoid construction had arrived faster on two feet than it could have crawled, the animated corpse was not speedy by any means, and its movements were relatively predictable. Besides, no matter how strong were the bonds between the zombie's various bits and pieces, Ox only needed to cut along the seams and they would fall and scatter.

Again Ox wondered, *What wish was so important that he was willing to make such a monstrosity of himself?*

The lurching, shuffling monster was nearly upon him now. Rabbit raised the blades that had served as his crutches.

Ox analyzed his attack. *No point in aiming for the vital parts, like the head or the heart. It wouldn't even give me any peace of mind.*

Instead, Ox focused entirely on dismantling the corpse. Before Rabbit could swing Shiro-usagi and Sangatsu-usagi down upon him, Ox's masterful slashes split the monster into six pieces—first the head, then the four limbs, and finally, he split the zombie's torso in two.

A corpse jumped out from the cleft.

Springing out at Ox like a grotesque jack-in-the-box was none other than Sharyū, the Fighter of the Monkey —once a hero, now a corpse. Ox grunted as she tackled him and took him to the ground with superhuman strength.

So, Monkey, you're already dead, Ox thought, realizing his fatal error.

His mistake wasn't failing to presume that Rabbit had killed the pacifist and turned her into his pawn. Ox lacked the information that could have enabled him to make that assumption. But he should have foreseen the possibility that some other corpse was hidden within the patchwork monster.

The gruesome sight of the model kit gone wrong distracted his thoughts from realizing it at the time. Because Rabbit had utilized some of his own body parts to hold the rest together from the outside, the golem should not have been the same size as Rabbit had been when he was alive; a hollow must have been inside there somewhere. If only Ox had realized there was a space for something else to occupy, he might have guessed that another of the necromanticist's minions—not necessarily Monkey, but somebody—was hiding within.

More likely than not, Rabbit hadn't simply been using the woman's body as filler to occupy the empty space—creating a place to hide her was the goal all along, so that when the unsuspecting Ox approached to cut him apart again, Monkey could pop out and catch him by surprise.

To say that they had caught him by surprise was understating it. He hadn't the slightest suspicion that another body could have been inside there. He had made a total and complete blunder. If only he hadn't let the gruesome sight distract his attention and cloud his thoughts...

No, even if I had managed to suspect another corpse was inside, the moment it turned out to be Monkey, my suspicions wouldn't have made any meaningful difference.

The dead hero pinned Ox down with unbelievable strength, preventing him from making the slightest movement. For being so small in stature—petite enough, after all, to have hidden inside the other corpse—Monkey possessed incredible raw physical power. Even accounting for the lack of inherent restraint all Rabbit's corpses shared, Ox was made painfully aware of just how much latent ability the pacifist had once kept bottled up—and was now being compelled to unleash.

While I fled with Tiger on my back, Rabbit summoned Monkey and joined their bodies together. He'd done such a horrifying mess of reshaping himself because appearing like a normal human hadn't been his goal. He wanted to construct a vessel in which to hide a human body, like prehistoric man once built houses out of mammoth bones.

Ox remained calm and analyzed his situation, not because the master had time to spare, and not because careful thinking could find him an opportunity to regain the upper hand. No, the Natural-Born Slayer was coming to terms with the reality that he had no way out.

When Monkey tackled him, his saber clattered to somewhere out of reach, and the slight-figured zombie had him completely pinned to the ground. She wasn't holding him in any kind of lock or hold; she was just that strong. If she had felt like it, she could have flattened his arms and legs into the pavement.

The only reason she didn't try to harm him was not because she had been a pacifist in life—it was because Ox had already been defeated. At the edge of his vision, Ox saw the pieces of Rabbit's corpse slowly reassemble. The process was going to take a little time, but with his prey captured, Rabbit could afford to take as long as he needed.

I see what he's doing, Ox thought in realization. *He doesn't want Monkey to kill me. He wants to kill me himself. He wants to gain control of me with as little damage done as possible.*

The future that Tiger had feared now bore down on Ox. He would become one of the walking dead, as had Boar, Dragon, Snake, and Monkey—or as some disfigured creature like Rabbit—stripped of consciousness, free will, or creed. He would keep on battling, following his leader's every command.

In that sense, it wouldn't be that much different from my life now. I'd still be a lowly soldier, just dead instead of alive—but I would no longer be doing the right things, and I don't want that.

Ox remembered what he had told the girl long ago. First, decide to do the right thing. Then do it. Now that he'd been bested, the words sounded so self-important.

Right now, the right thing is to do what? To kill myself? All I have to do is decide and do it.

Even if his arms and legs couldn't budge, he could still bite through his tongue, just as Rabbit had done. Of all the actions he could ever take, suicide seemed the least like who he was. But what other choice did he have?

Pain shot through his face.

Correctly sensing his determination—or rather, indecision—Monkey slammed her forehead against Ox's chin. With a single head-butt, she had prevented Ox's suicide—by shattering his teeth.

Without teeth, he couldn't bite through his tongue—although in truth, he might not have been able to go through with the deed. Either way, she had removed the option by using the least possible force and doing the least possible damage.

I suppose losing all my teeth won't make any difference when I'm a mute zombie. I don't use them as a weapon either—though I doubt losing them will help my looks.

The taste of iron filled his mouth. *The moment Monkey's corpse fell into Rabbit's clutches, the Zodiac War might have been as good as over. I don't know how many other fighters are still alive, but I don't think Dog or Sheep will be able to put up much resistance.*

Who else was there? There should have been one more. The pain in Ox's mouth made it hard to gather his thoughts. Then, as the recollection began to form, a voice spoke.

"I am Nezumi, the Fighter of the Rat. I kill inexorably."

That's right, the Rat. Ox turned his head in the direction of the voice. Standing there was the boy who had appeared sleepy from the beginning and still appeared sleepy now. The youth seemed too young to be a fighter—though Ox, who had seen his first battle at the age of five, was hardly the person to judge whether or not the boy was too young.

Why had he come? Ox had seen no trace of him in the war. Why should he make his appearance now? The battle was all but wrapped up, and the boy could do nothing to change it. There was being in the wrong place, and there was this. It was almost laughable.

The boy had shown up as if to save Ox from certain death, but surely that wasn't the case. No one—save for the drunken Tiger—would be so foolish as to come to the rescue of the Natural-Born Slayer.

"Looks like I'm not too late," the boy said. "Finding Sheep's body took me longer than I thought it would. Well, I wasn't trying to find his body exactly. I was trying to find these."

The boy held out a handful of grenades—the Shūkaiokuri that Hitsujii, the Sheep, had brought into the fight—weapons so destructive that even Monkey had feared them.

2

Rabbit's corpse was gradually but steadily piecing itself back together, but until it had finished, it couldn't go anywhere. Monkey had Ox pinned down, but she couldn't move without releasing him.

The boy had said he wasn't too late, when in truth he was perfectly on time. This was the only moment that could have worked—this specific timing and none other. Never again would the opportunity arise to eliminate both Rabbit's and Monkey's corpses at once. Of course, Ox would be eliminated with them, but he had already accepted his death.

Ox didn't know what kind of person Rat was or how the boy had managed to get there. He didn't know—or care—if Rat was the most dastardly villain on Earth, who had watched and waited for his chance out of pure cowardice. What mattered was that the boy came bearing weapons perhaps more suited than any other for destroying the undead.

"I'm not sure this will give you any peace of mind," the boy said, "but I was only able to bring these grenades here because Tiger killed Sheep. Everything that's about to happen is thanks to your ally. Now, do you have any final words?"

"No," Ox said without hesitation. "Just do it."

Even if Rat were the world's worst villain, even if he were a coward, Ox felt certain he'd rather have the boy win than let Rabbit walk free. He could imagine no worse future than one where the necromanticist, with Ox's and Monkey's corpses in tow, went from battlefield to battlefield creating zombies en masse.

Ox would decide to do right, then he would do it—just as Tiger had done as he took her life.

He said, "To me, this is what's right. Spend your life doing what you believe is right."

He closed his eyes.

"I am Ushii, the Fighter of the Ox. I just kill."

After Ox announced himself, Rat paused in silence, then rolled all his grenades into the group and quickly distanced himself. Ox saw how Rat could have survived—the boy could run with terrific speed.

Now that I think about it, when the Jade Emperor created the zodiac, the rat claimed the first spot by hitching a ride on an ox.

What happened here wasn't all that different from the legend, but Ox didn't mind it happening to him. The boy's attempt at giving him peace of mind had been a bit of a stretch, but it had proved surprisingly effective. Winning the Zodiac War seemed unimportant now, and he felt no regret conceding to the boy.

What will he wish for? Ox wondered. *And why do I get the feeling I've met him somewhere before?*

The grenades exploded.

The former arms dealer's implied threat on the observation deck had been no lie or exaggeration. With far more destructive power than seemed possible from objects that fit in the palm of a hand, the explosion disintegrated Monkey, Rabbit, and Ox, and even the nearby Tiger, along with everything else in the area. All that remained were the eleven murky-black jewels they had once held.

Added to the one carried by Rat, who had taken shelter back in the sewers, that made twelve.

The Twelfth Zodiac War had ended.

RAT VS. ~~OX~~

END OF THE 11ᵀᴴ BATTLE

WAR'S END

"The mountain brought forth a mouse."

NEZUMI,
THE FIGHTER
OF THE RAT

"I wish to dream."

REAL NAME: **Tsugiyoshi SUMINO**
BORN: **March 3**
HEIGHT: **170 cm**
WEIGHT: **55 kg**

Tsugiyoshi is a soldier and a high school student. His most prominent ability in battle, the Hundred Paths of Nezumi-san, allows him to tamper with the realm of probability. Tsugiyoshi can carry out a hundred different choices at once, then select which course of events becomes reality. For example, if he were playing rock-paper-scissors, he could throw rock, paper, and scissors at the same time. Should he settle on rock, then reality acts as if he never tried paper or scissors.

If you considered the power as predicting the future one hundred different ways and then selecting one of them, you'd be fairly close, but for two major differences: the predictions are based on actions of his choosing, and he experiences every one.

If time is like a flowchart, he can test one hundred of its forked paths, then choose whichever route he likes the best. This may seem a bit like cheating, but most paths end up being largely similar, and simultaneously experiencing one hundred potential realities comes with a heavy mental burden—in other words, it's exhausting.

The discarded paths are remembered only by him (with some exceptions), but he doesn't have perfect recall—one hundred different experiences make for too much to retain completely.

Another major downside is the potential for experiencing a hundred times more failures. He can confess his feelings to a crush in one hundred different ways and be spurned each and every time. (Once, he had to suffer through being dumped one hundred times simultaneously.)

Ultimately, Tsugiyoshi considers his ability not much good for anything except playing rock-paper-scissors—but he was chosen for the Zodiac War despite his young age because he possessed a hundred times more combat experience than typically afforded by the actual number of battles he'd seen. He tried to escape being selected for the Zodiac War, but of the hundred paths, not even one was successful.

His experiences have taught him that there is no one correct path in life, and that even if the concept of truth exists, there's no one right answer. This learning has given him a distinctly philosophical personality.

The only time he gets excited is when he's eating cheese—no two cheeses taste the same.

1

"Congratulations, Fighter Nezumi. You are the winner of the Twelfth Zodiac War. Everybody, clap your hands!"

The judge, Duodecuple, vigorously applauded. "Everyone" didn't join in—not, as in the opening ceremony, because no one felt like it, but because there was no one left to clap.

In a small, dreary reception office on anther floor in the same high-rise, Nezumi, the Fighter of the Rat, sat absently listening to the judge speak.

Duodecuple said, "We've neutralized the poison. The jewel will dissolve in your stomach without any trace or harmful effect."

"That's good," Rat said. "Can I go home now?"

"Not yet. Your presence is required just a little longer." Duodecuple chuckled. "After all, that was a brilliant victory. We'd like to conduct a short interview for posterity's sake. I'm sure you understand."

More like an interrogation, Rat thought, rubbing his tired head. He used his power to refuse the questioning in a hundred different ways, but all attempts failed—and forty ended with him getting killed. It seemed there was no getting out of this.

Compared to what I just went through—getting killed ninety-nine times out of a hundred—a sixty percent survival rate is nothing to worry about.

Of the sixty where he remained alive, he chose a route that preserved a relatively amicable atmosphere between him and the old man. The potential route became the reality.

Rat said, "Well, what do you want to ask?"

"First, I'd like to hear you explain the actions you took during the war. With your particular talent, no one outside yourself could observe your behavior, or its results, which leaves us no opportunity to study or judge your deeds. We need to hear it from you, if you'll be so kind."

Annoyed by the old man's insincere, patronizing attitude, Rat lunged at Duodecuple to give the judge a good beating— at the same time as he obediently answered, "I didn't do anything that unusual."

Rat decided to make the latter choice in reality, since the first path ended with him being dead so fast he didn't know what killed him.

Rat continued. "I just did what I always do, and I tried a hundred different strategies at once. One simply happened to work. I got lucky, that's all."

"I see, I see," Duodecuple said, smiling happily for some reason. "No matter how superior the fighter, be they hero or prodigy—or corpse even—they get to take only one course of action. Whatever they decide, whatever they do, they can't turn left and right at the same time. But you, Fighter Nezumi, with your unique power over probability, you can. In this Zodiac War, we were graced with a variety of competitors who possessed unusual talents, but now that it's over, it's clear you managed an overwhelming victory."

That's easy for you to say, Rat thought.

"That's easy for you to say," Rat said simultaneously.

Neither resulted in a remarkable difference, and he chose the reality where he kept the thought to himself.

Do you have any idea how hard it is to carry out a hundred different battles at once? Ah, I'm so unbelievably tired right now.

He didn't merely desire sleep, he felt as if his mind was being chipped away. All this constant, ceaseless thinking was beginning to seriously affect his ability to stay conscious. He just wanted to go home. He wanted to go home and sleep. He suspected that being more cooperative would get this over with more quickly and tested ten different levels of cooperation to see which was most effective.

Duodecuple continued, "You're like Schrödinger's cat. Inside the box, the cat is both dead and alive—although I suppose you would be Schrödinger's rat. You know, that reminds me about a story of how the zodiac was created. They say the reason there's no cat in the zodiac is because Rat tricked him."

Rat suspected this bit of small talk was intended to loosen his lips.

The judge added, "Although this time, you could say that Rat got rid of all the other animals."

"I think there is a cat in the zodiac," Rat said. "Tigers are like cats, aren't they?"

"They are indeed," Duodecuple said, nodding agreeably.

Rat thought about Tiger. In the branch he chose, he hadn't encountered her at all, but in others, the two rivals had joined forces.

We weren't bad as a team, Rat thought. *But Ox and Tiger were wicked strong. In the end, I basically rode their coat tails... But I owe someone else even more.*

Rat said, "Of the hundred strategies I came up with by

wracking my inferior mind, this is the only path where I won—
and I owe it to Sharyū more than anything I thought up."

"Oh?" the judge said.

Of all the ways Rat tried his previous response, this was the
way that most drew Duodecuple's interest, and Rat went with
it. This questioning had him feeling as if he were walking on
thin ice. *It seems my battle isn't yet over*, he thought.

That kind of thinking only depressed him. Instead, he
went with a path where he hadn't thought so hard about it.

Rat said, "It was something she told me in the sewers after
Chicken warned us about the necromanticist. Sharyū told me
that if she ever died and was brought under the necromanticist's control, she wanted me to kill her."

Duodecuple's smile deepened here, as it had in every path
Rat investigated. Ultimately, the boy's powers were limited,
and often all his choices found the same result—much like
the ninety-nine of one hundred attempts at the Zodiac War
that resulted in his death. This power, no matter how highly
Duodecuple lauded it, fundamentally existed for the sole purpose of showing Rat how powerless he was. In order to survive, he died ninety-nine times. When thought of as a process
of trial and error, his victory might seem a product of effort
and perseverance, but a more accurate description would be
to say that of one hundred Rats, ninety-nine died. His deaths
had been erased along with the paths that contained them,
remaining only in Rat's memories.

In what way could ninety-nine deaths be considered a victory? It couldn't. It was a pitiful defeat. Rat felt no victor's ela-
tion after the Zodiac War. Everyone else had only died once,
while he died ninety-nine times.

Can you even imagine what it's like to live a life where you can't make any excuses like, I should have done this or I should have done that? I can try anything I think of, only to learn I still fail. Ox said to do what I believe is right, but I don't believe that anything is right. Look what happened this time…

Rat said, "I told her I wouldn't do it. I learned how strong she was in the routes where I was unlucky enough to fight her. But then she told me that Sheep's high explosives—the ones he mentioned when we were being told the rules—would work well against the undead. She said she could manage them alive, but not dead."

And she had been right. Rat had told Ox that killing Rabbit was thanks to Tiger, but it was also thanks to Monkey. By that measure, Ox also played a role by keeping the former pacifist occupied—otherwise, she might have escaped the grenades.

Sharyū claimed she didn't know who intended to attack the entire group at the beginning, but I bet she suspected Sheep—she just didn't want to say it if she wasn't absolutely sure.

Rat continued, "The point is, all the strategies I came up with on my own failed. Like I said, it was luck. This was the only path where the course of the contest happened to take shape in a way that benefited me."

"You're being too humble," Duodecuple said. "You were able to respond admirably well to a battle that was in a state of constant and bewildering change. I imagine that experiencing one hundred branching paths at once helps you react so quickly, but it's still impressive."

"By the way," Rat said, "Sharyū never told me her plan for a peaceful resolution in any of my paths."

Had the pacifist only been bluffing, as Rat had speculated to Horse in the bank vault?

Duodecuple chuckled. "Even still, I wouldn't be so sure she was making it up. For example, I can imagine a scenario in which she knew some of what goes on behind the Zodiac War." The judge let this slip in only three of Rat's hundred scenarios. "Rather than use her single wish directly, she might have intended on using it to negotiate with the organizers. That hero and savior of nations had deep connections with many states. Sitting at the big table with *them*, betting countries—I could see her dealing with them on equal terms."

Betting countries? The big table? Them?

Rat didn't know what the man was talking about. No matter how many paths he could follow, he was only one little rodent, and such secrets were not to be his—neither could he know the hero's true intentions. He had no information-gathering ability like the Eye of the Cormorant, and his hundred-fold experience would never compare with that of a true veteran.

All I can do with my possibilities is scurry around, and if I can't be perceptive enough to make good of it, then I'm nothing, Rat thought, though with not much sentimentality.

As for Rat's scurrying, Horse had thought it incredible that the boy had managed to penetrate the barricaded bank vault, but there wasn't anything incredible about it. Rat simply put his Hundred Paths ability to use.

As Horse himself had been aware, any barricade, no matter how sturdy, was still a product of haste—some gap would exist somewhere. Finding that gap, however, required time. Rat had searched the piled-up debris from one hundred different approaches and found an opening. To put it another way, Rat commanded one hundred searchers to find Horse's mistake.

And finding the cracks is a rat's specialty—of my hundred attempts, about ten found an entrance large enough for me to slip through.

This, too, was a stunt of little practical use, and one that counted on someone else making a mistake. In this instance, however, it had allowed him to escape Snake and Monkey's pursuit.

Rat said, "If Sharyū wasn't bluffing, then I can only take that to mean I didn't have what it took to be a part of it. I hope that she would have pulled it off in one of the routes where I died. She said she had many different plans—I pray that each had a path to be successful."

Prayer wouldn't change the fact that he had erased all other possibilities. In that sense, just as Monkey had saved more people than any other fighter, then Rat killed more than any other fighter—or, he had killed entire worlds by wiping them from existence.

Duodecuple chuckled again. "Peaceful resolutions or not, I wonder who won in each of those other ninety-nine paths."

Rat would have liked to know that himself, but each of those paths ended in his death and left him no knowledge of what happened after—though he seriously doubted any scenario ended with Monkey's peace.

In any case, no route contained all twelve fighters, including myself, joining hands and finding another way—or at least, no route that led from my first choice.

Judging from everything he experienced up until his deaths, Rat guessed that Rabbit won the majority of the time, followed by Ox and Tiger. Dog's and Sheep's bending of the rules—or outright breaking of them—rarely paid off. Maybe that meant that a straightforward approach was the best policy—except Rat might have been the least straightforward of all.

"By the way," Rat said, "among the hundred patterns, there was one where Rabbit and I came to a mutually beneficial arrangement. When I built up the courage to speak to him, we found more common ground than I'd have thought. Our partnership ended when I screwed up and got both of us killed by Horse."

Working with Rabbit was an experience that was hard to come by. Rat didn't retain a perfect recollection of all his experiences, but that one had left a vivid impression.

Rat said, "It wasn't just him either. Aside from Sharyū, they were all scoundrels—but when I tried talking to the others, they were shockingly open with me. I didn't know what to think of that. I scurried around asking everyone what they would wish for, and the ones who told me had wishes that were…I don't know how to put it—normal, or common, maybe? I was surprised at how modest their wishes were."

"I see," Duodecuple said.

Rat was taken aback. He felt like the judge had gotten him to spill everything—even though the boy had long felt he should never speak of the alternate paths he'd erased. Rat felt like he had failed, and he supposed that meant Duodecuple had succeeded. The boy considered erasing this path, but in every other simultaneous conversation with the judge, Rat always ended up talking. His power was not unlimited.

Besides, I don't think I can handle being any more exhausted than this.

As if reading the boy's thoughts, Duodecuple said, "Thank you for your cooperation. I have no further questions. What you've told me today will inform the next Zodiac War twelve years from now. Now, go back home and have a good rest. Whenever you decide how you want to spend your single wish, please get in touch with me. I am at your disposal."

Duodecuple bowed deeply. "You say the other fighters' wishes were modest. I look forward to seeing how majestic yours will be."

Rat said, "That's a good point. As long as there's no rush, I'll take my time thinking it over."

Rat made a show of standing up. He didn't feel any tremendous pressure over choosing the right wish, but if he did it now, he might just wish to go to sleep. He had no intention of seeking any deep meaning from this battle, but that would have been too much of a waste.

"Anyway," Rat said, "I'll make my wish after I've thought of a hundred."

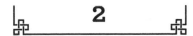

2

The next day, the boy went to the school that was just another battlefield to him. There, as he lived one hundred lives, he thought of the one wish he really wanted to come true—and the ninety-nine others he didn't so much.

END OF THE ZODIAC WAR

AFTERWORD

Coming to the realization that I didn't actually know the origins of the Chinese zodiac had a chilling effect on me. Realizing one's own ignorance can have that effect, but in this case, what I found disturbing was how, in the festive time of the new year, I'd say things like, "It's the year of the Snake," or "the year of the Boar," despite not knowing the origin of what I was saying. Astrology and blood-type divination share a similar distinction. Without knowing the root of these beliefs, we regard them as customs that just somehow sprouted into our shared culture. We accept them as conventional knowledge, but when you think about it, there's nothing conventional about them, and when you really think about it, it's really scary. (Although I suppose another way to look at it is that most things work out even if you don't know their workings.)

Knowledge and common knowledge stand across a divide yet remain compatible with each other. It's likely that what we think of as the zodiac in the present day is completely different than it was when it was created, and yet we feel no discord—much as the differences between two landscapes don't stand out unless you directly compare the views. Along those lines, creating an original zodiac from scratch might be fun, but the result would be too incongruous. That said, I think whoever decided to put Rat in the first slot had the right idea.

This novel is the story of twelve fighters who bear the names of the zodiac. Matters are complicated along the way, but leaving those roots aside, at the basic level I depicted fighters who battle because they accept that's the way things are, without their understanding the reason they fight—if they even have one.

We all have asked ourselves, I'm sure, what we would wish for if we had just one wish. Perhaps when people are asking themselves that, they aren't asking what they want, but rather they're asking what they lack. Is not our karma to want what we lack? When someone has something they feel they don't need, and another person doesn't have that thing and wants it, that's the basis of supply and demand. If twelve people were to come together, I feel like they could find a way to barter with each other. I wonder what these twelve could have done to reach that outcome instead. Along those lines, what is your wish?

By the way, the follow-up to this story is included in a manga anthology called *Ōgiri*. Despite the manga being a follow-up, I actually wrote it first. I would love for you to read that as well. Hikaru Nakamura's captivating character designs brought this story to my mind and reaffirmed to me the power illustrations contain. One reason I wrote this book was because I hoped that Nakamura Sensei could draw its cover, and I extend my deepest gratitude to her along with the editorial department at Shueisha's j BOOKS imprint who made this book a reality. Everybody clap your hands!

—NISIOISIN

APPENDIX
CHARACTER NAME MEANINGS

*(Note: the kanji for zodiac figures
differs from the typical animal names.)*

BOAR (亥)
Toshiko INŌ 伊能淑子
Inōnoshishi 異能肉 (肉)

Inō (いのう・異能) means superpower.

Shishi (しし・肉) means meat or flesh [of wild game such as boar].

Inoshishi (いのしし・猪) means wild boar.

Her name means "boar with superpowers" with an added suggestion that she dwells on matters of the flesh.

DOG (戌)
Michio TSUKUI 津久井道雄
Dokku 怒突 (怒)

Do (ど・怒) represents anger.

Doku (毒) means poison.

Tsuku (つく・突く) means to prick or to stab (or perhaps, to bite with a sharp fang); to strike; to attack at a weakness or by surprise.

Doggu (どっぐ) is how the English word "dog" is transliterated into Japanese.

His name means "mad dog that makes cunning use of his sharp fangs."

CHICKEN (酉)
Ryōka NIWA 丹羽遼香
Niwatori 庭取 (庭)

Niwa (にわ・庭) represents a partitioned space, most usually a garden or courtyard, but also a field or area of action: 家庭 for a household or 戦いの庭 for a battlefield.

Tori (とり・取り) means taking/claiming.

Tori (とり・鳥) means bird.

Niwatori (にわとり・鶏) means chicken.

The reference to gardens also ties into her favored weapon, a spading fork she calls Cockscomb.

Her name means, "chicken who claims the field."

In Japanese, the character 酉 is gender-neutral.

MONKEY (申)
Misaki YŪKI 柚木美咲
Sharyū 砂粒 (砂)

Sha (しゃ・砂) is a variant reading for sand.

Ryū (りゅう・粒) represents grains of a substance.

The combination sounds quite similar to *saru* (さる・猿), the word for monkey.

SHEEP (未)
Sumihiko TSUJIIE 辻家純彦
Hitsujii 必爺(必)

Hitsu (ひつ・必) means certainty.

Jii (じい・爺) means old man.

Hitsuji (ひつじ・羊) means sheep.

HORSE (午)
Yoshimi SŌMA 早間好美
Uuma 迂々真(々)

U (う・迂) represents a roundabout way or detour, as well as carelessness and ignorance.

The second character (々) is a shorthand representation for a repeated character, and is sometimes referred to as *noma* (のま), which is a homonym with a word for pasture-kept horse.

Ma (ま・真) represents truth, genuineness, and sincerity.

Uma (馬) means horse.

His name means "horse that is careless and naïve but earnest."

SNAKE (巳)
Takeyasu TSUMITA 積田剛保
Tatsumi Brother, the Younger 断罪兄弟・弟 (断罪弟)

Tatsu (たつ・断つ) means to sever.

Tsumi (つみ・罪) means crime, wrongdoing; or punishment.

When combined they can be read as *danzai* (だんざい・断罪), which means judgment or conviction of a crime; or beheading.

Tatsu (たつ・辰) is also the word for the Dragon in the zodiac, while *mi* (み・巳) is the word for Snake in the zodiac; the two combined can be read as Dragon and Snake.

Tatsumi is also their family name *Tsumita* written in reverse.

Otōto (おとうと・弟) means younger brother.

DRAGON (辰)
Nagayuki TSUMITA 積田長幸
Tatsumi Brother, the Elder 断罪兄弟・兄 (断罪兄)

Same as above, but *ani* (あに・兄) means elder brother.

RABBIT (卯)
name unknown
Usagi 憂城 (憂)

Usa (うさ・憂さ) means gloom, melancholy, or lingering sadness.

Ki (き・城) means a walled-in fortress or keep. (When used in a compound the *ki* sound can become voiced: *gi*.)

Usagi (うさぎ・兔) means rabbit.

His name means "lonesome rabbit."

TIGER (寅)
Kanae AIRA 始良香奈江
Tora 妬良 (良)

To (と・妬) represents envy or jealousy.

Ra (ら・良) represents good (in quality or nature), skilled, or kind.

Tora (とら・虎) means tiger.

OX (丑)
Eiji KASHII 樫井栄児
Ushii 失井 (失)

Ushinau (うしなう・失う) means to lose something (tangible or intangible) or someone; to fail.

I (い・井) means a well or waterhole.

Ushi (うし・牛) means cow, ox, or bull.

RAT (子)
Tsugiyoshi SUMINO 墨野継義
Nezumi 寝住 (住)

Ne (ね・寝) means sleep.

Sumi (すみ・住み) means to reside or dwell in. (When used in a compound the *su* sound can become voiced: *zu*.)

Nezumi (ねずみ・鼠) means rat.

His name means "a rat that occupies the state of sleep."

JUNI TAISEN: ZODIAC WAR

JUUNI TAISEN © 2015 by NISIOISIN, Hikaru Nakamura
All rights reserved.
First published in Japan in 2015 by SHUEISHA Inc., Tokyo.
English translation rights arranged by SHUEISHA Inc.

Cover and interior design by Adam Grano
Translation by Nathan A. Collins

Published by
VIZ Media, LLC
P.O. Box 77010
San Francisco, CA 94107
www.viz.com

Library of Congress Cataloging-in-Publication Data

Names: Nishio, Ishin, 1981- author. | Nakamura, Hikaru, 1984- illustrator. |
    Collins, Nathan, translator.
Title: Juni Taisen : zodiac war / story by Nisioisin ; illustrations by
    Hikaru Nakamura ; translated by Nathan A. Collins.
Other titles: Juni Taisen. English
Description: San Francisco : VIZ Media, [2017] | Series: Juni taisen: zodiac war
Identifiers: LCCN 2017031743 | ISBN 9781421597508 (hardback)
Subjects: | BISAC: FICTION / Media Tie-In. | FICTION / Fantasy /
    Contemporary. | COMICS & GRAPHIC NOVELS / Manga / Media Tie-In.
Classification: LCC PL873.5.I84 J8613 2017 | DDC 895.63/6--dc23
LC record available at https://lccn.loc.gov/2017031743

Printed in the U.S.A.
First printing, October 2017